HARVEST OF

THE DAMNED

To Jackie

With all good Wishes.

JESS LAMBERT

Jess Lambert 24-01-2011

Published by

MELROSE BOOKS

An Imprint of Melrose Press Limited
St Thomas Place, Ely
Cambridgeshire
CB7 4GG, UK
www.melrosebooks.com

FIRST EDITION

Cover designed by Jeremy Kay

ISBN 978 1 907040 67 2

Printed and bound in Great Britain by:
CPI Anthony Rowe. Chippenham, Wiltshire

FSC
www.fsc.org
MIX
Paper from
responsible sources
FSC® C013604

FOREWORD

T HIS IS A STORY OF GREAT TENACITY and professionalism and concerns a small group of recruits conscripted for National Service during the Second World War. There were many groups like this one, ordinary men, from ordinary backgrounds, tasked to do extraordinary deeds. They did not seek adventure, rather it was thrust upon them and they were not found wanting… these quiet heroes.

My group joined the Royal Marines and upon completion of their training were selected, where suitable, to train as Commandos prior to setting sail for an unknown destination.

Embarking upon a journey to the unknown, my story accompanies these men to and through India, and on to their ultimate destination, Burma, where they came under the umbrella of the Fourteenth Army, which ultimately became known as 'The Forgotten Army'.

Due to the prioritisation of the war in Europe and the focussed press attention, naturally, on the Normandy landings, it wasn't until the war in Europe was seen to be progressing to a satisfactory conclusion that the famous Churchillian rhetoric was unleashed upon that important war in the east, that to a degree had been fought in anonymity and hardly recognised. Winston Churchill turned his attention and acerbic tongue to the matters persisting in the east and, recognising the sterling work and extreme bravery of the fighting forces in Burma, he labelled them the 'Never to be forgotten Army', a name to stand proudly alongside the 'Desert Rats' and 'The Few', names that were earned through shed blood and a Herculean determination of those involved to succeed against all expectations.

Under the cover of a major assault on the village of Kangaw a section of Marines trekked inland, on foot, on a covert operation in an effort to destroy the Japanese oil production capabilities and storage facilities situated on the far side of the An mountain range (the spinal backbone that is the backdrop of the Arakan Peninsula). This was an important target and this mission needed to proceed to prevent the retreating Japanese army from mounting a 'Dunkirk' down one of the few metalled roads and waterways of the Irrawaddi.

This account describes the problems and difficulties of twenty men who set out to trek to, and through the high An Pass of the Arakan Yoma in order to fulfil their mission to reach and destroy their twin objectives. Many men died in the fighting around the production rigs; only one wounded man made it back to base to report their target destroyed, whilst the small force who attacked the storage facility withdrew in good order, having succeeded in their mission.

Stung by the scale of the attacks the Japanese relentlessly pursued the fragmented British force through jungle and over mountain, motivated only by vengeance.

The retreat through enemy territory hounded by the Japanese force was a daunting and costly flight.

Of the twenty men who set out only a handful survived.

Author's Note

THE CHARACTERS THAT PEOPLE THIS BOOK AND accompany me on this five year journey are entirely of my own creation, and bear no resemblance to any person – living or dead. Although they have been endowed with all the good qualities of the men I served with in this theatre of war.

If I have inadvertently used any of the names of the men who actually served on the Arakan Front I apologise to them for so doing.

Certain historical figures and events are mentioned together with the factual settings; these however are purely to provide a 'Window in Time', through which these events may be viewed.

It is set in a period when British and American fortunes were possibly at their lowest ebb during the Second World War. It is not the intention to comment on, embellish or denigrate the contributions made, only to refer with honour, gratitude and pride to the selfless achievements of this generation of service personnel, to whom we owe our todays, and doubtless all our tomorrows.

Royal Marines

An' after I met 'im all over the World,
a-doin' all kinds of things,
Like landin' 'isself with a Gatlin' gun
to talk to them 'eathen Kings;

****

But they're camped an' fed, an' they're
Up an' fed before our bugle's blew.
Ho! they ain't no limpin' procrastitutes – Soldier an' Sailor
too.

****

There ain't a job on the top of the earth
The beggars don't know, nor do –
You can land 'im at night on a bald man's head
To paddle his own canoe –
'E's a sort of a bloomin' cosmopolouse –
Soldier an' Sailor too.

****

Rudyard Kipling.

To Joan, Aladdin's Lamp Was Mine

****

Here with a Loaf of Bread beneath the Bough,
A Flask of Wine, A Book of Verse – and Thou
Beside me singing in the Wilderness – And,
Wilderness is Paradise Enow!

From: **The Rubaiyat of Omar Khayyam**

ONE

NOVEMBER WAS NOT A MONTH IN WHICH to go sailing.

The southwesterly gale which bore up from the Firth of Clyde made the bleak waters of the Greenock anchorage rave with countless whitecaps. The edges of the wave crests began to break into spindrift, the long fingers of foam being blown along the direction of the wind in well-marked streaks, whilst the following troughs were whipped up as spray at the height of their frenzy and driven far into the distant hills, scarifying the land and flattening the gorse and heather like a vast sea of wet grain.

The lights that fringed the shore and those of the crofters' cottages further inland blinked momentarily before being obscured by the flurries of sleet, and even the majestic pines tossed their heads and made deep obeisance before this onslaught of nature.

The peacetime cruise liner the *Athlone Castle*, who had spent the bulk of her commissions sailing warmer climes, lay tethered to No. 4 Wharf like some skittish filly, prancing and bucking to the dictates of the weather. Her bow, waist and stern lines snatched alternately at her giant restraints.

The single light that spilled from the darkened ship was from the captain's day cabin, giving the grey mass the appearance of a Cyclops.

The atmosphere on board was warm and friendly, and even though the luxury fittings had been torn out to make way for the mess decks the troopship, as she now was, could not completely conceal the splendour of her former trade, and like her sister ship the *Sterling Castle* and many of their contemporaries called up for the duration her superiority seemed incongruous and out of place.

Her whole appearance was that of an aging dowager who had seen better days, the drab grey wartime dress blending in perfectly with her surroundings.

The only sound above the weather was the complaining creak of her mooring lines as she responded to the goad of the sea, rubbing herself fondly against the huge rope fenders, and the steel-tipped footfalls of the armed sentries as they paced their beat down the length of the wharf, the weather forcing them to lean alternately into the driving wind and sleet and then turn, pausing only briefly to exchange some obscenity before being driven forward again by that same unrelenting hand.

The dockyard lights suspended some thirty foot above and around the perimeter of the wharf, their radiance reduced to a mere token by the masking imposed by the wartime blackout restrictions, added to the sad and forlorn air of an empty stage.

This illusion was further emphasised by the pools of water that lay around the uneven surface of the dockyard, which seemed to catch and reflect them back as impoverished footlights, setting the stage for the next act of a continuing saga which had seen an exultant German army tightening its grip on a shocked and cowering Europe.

Hitler's regime, by force of arms, had made him the master of eight European capitals: Warsaw, Copenhagen, Oslo, The Hague, Brussels, Paris, Belgrade and Athens.

The English Channel, which for centuries had proved a defensive moat against the envy of more ambitious nations, had once again temporarily halted the might of a would-be invader.

Hitler had become the ruler of Europe from the Arctic to semi-tropical Crete, and his armies were unbeaten even further south to the borders of Egypt.

Britain now stood alone. Facing her across the channel, around the ports a mere twenty miles away, was massed the might of the Wehrmacht, who during their Blitzkreig to within sight of the 'White Cliffs' had badly mauled the British Expeditionary Force that had landed in France with such high hopes.

The only saving grace had been the miraculous evacuation by sea of some 340,000 men from the beaches of Dunkirk. These must now be rested and absorbed into the various units, to form a nucleus of seasoned veterans to once again take the fight across the Channel.

Germany's decision not to follow up their success was inexplicable, but the lull – however brief – was to Britain's advantage, allowing it time to recover and consolidate its battered battalions.

Failure to gain mastery of the air over Britain and the Channel caused Hitler to override his generals, and probably paying more attention to his soothsayer he turned his face towards the east and launched Operation Barbarossa, the invasion of Russia.

This vast country, history has shown, could swallow whole armies, and this decision could only be to Britain's advantage.

Two

LIEUTENANT COMMANDER GEOFFREY BRIDGES, A TALL MAN of indeterminate age, with a mop of flaming red hair that completely belied his nature, leaned back wearily in his swivel chair and pushed the well-worn folder away from him across the desk. Reaching for his favourite pipe, he filled it, packed it down with the heel of his thumb, lit it, and puffed away contentedly.

With eyes half-closed he watched as the smoke curled towards the deck-head of his cabin before being sucked out through the half-opened scuttle and smiled to himself with satisfaction as the air became drenched with the aroma of Erinmore Rub.

Half rising from his chair he dropped the slim tobacco pouch and lighter into the pocket of a coat which hung at the bottom of his bunk.

His recently cleaned coat, the sleeve of which sported the two and a half wavy lines of gold braid told of his rank. The Royal Naval Volunteer Reserves were the amateurs who had become professionals because of the tremendous losses sustained by the regulars during the first few months of the war. He smiled grimly to himself as he recalled the centuries old trueism,

God and the Navy we adore

When danger threatens but not before

It had taken a war to find that he was needed again. Pleasure boats and paddle steamers being pressed into service as minesweepers. Obsolete First World War destroyers having to fight both the Atlantic and a modern German navy. Similarly with the Royal Air Force, totally unprepared, with not more than a handful of planes to go against Goering's Luftwaffe. The powers that be pursuing appeasement and signing what would be proved later to be worthless pieces of paper.

A government without foresight or leadership, preferring to keep able-bodied men in the soul-destroying dole queues, unwilling to create work and to spend to enable Britain to stand alongside more ambitious nations.

With furrowed brows he again contemplated his recent task, the problem of victualling and conveying 1,500 service personnel to the other side of the globe.

That he was equal to the task he felt confident enough to take for granted; perhaps the real trouble was with this exact moment in history.

At the start of the First World War, he had been too young to be involved with any fighting, but like many of his generation, he had cursed his lack of years as he watched his father and elder brothers answer the country's call. Now he was wondering if he was not too old to play any useful part in the second round against the same enemy.

What the politicians had done with the intervening years of peace had left him with a decidedly jaundiced view of his fellow man, particularly with those perennial non-combatant fat cats who treated the common soldier as units to be expended.

His own considered view was that politicians both local and national, like babies' napkins, should be changed regularly, and for the same reason.

When the Earl Haig was once reputed to have said to his officers during a briefing, "I can afford to expend 250,000 units on the next assault on the Western Front," it took some time for it to sink in that the units he was referring to were men.

'Lions lead by donkeys' would take a lot of generations to live down.

Sinking further back into his chair, it seemed that he was looking down upon himself wondering whether or not he was dreaming, for this command had come out of the blue. In 1928 after nine years' service, as a result of Britain's maritime winding down and decay, Bridges had become one of the many victims of the Admiralty axe.

He had spent the next three soul-destroying years on the beach, and then the next eight on rust buckets and banana boats in the Far East, plying monotonously and seemingly endlessly between palm-fringed islands.

With only two commands in that period he did not consider it a very good recommendation for a wartime appointment, although the last three years in coastal craft might count for something, for after all it was only a case of follow my leader. These wartime convoys were evenly spaced and vulnerable to long-range aircraft and U-boats; even the zigzag routes were ultimately predictable as the destinations were obvious.

The officers and crew he was not worried about at all. Naval training and discipline died very hard, and the ingrained habit and tradition coupled with the natural pride in the Senior Service would manifest itself whenever required.

Coming suddenly down to earth Bridges mentally avowed that any doubts he had must not show; he must be concise and confident at all times, because this attitude was all important. Confidence and ability should naturally be infectious and spread from the top. Too late now for second thoughts.

The ship sat low and fat, key ratings and advance parties were already on board and tomorrow the main body of troops would arrive. The route they would take was already plotted; the rest was in the lap of the gods.

In the meantime, he had to arrange to entertain the colonel and adjutant of the thousand odd army personnel who were due to take passage to India, together with the marine captain and second-in-command of the LCM Flotilla who were also to be his concern.

The wardroom table was laid and the naval stewards stood with napkins over their arms waiting for the officers to be seated.

Bridges opened the procedure with introductions.

"I am Lieutenant Commander. Bridges, Captain of the *Athlone Castle*. My Number One, Lieutenant Price; my Number Two, Sub-Lieutenant Stanway; Signals Officer, Lieutenant Savage; Surgeon, Lieutenant Clifford; engineering, Lieutenant Maynard; and our junior, Sub-Lieutenant Cordingly. And now we come to our reason for being here. On my left are Colonel J P Jeffers and his adjutant Captain P Smithers, who will be bringing their army contingent, and Captain Newsome and his adjutant Lieutenant C Parry who will be accompanying the Marine Commando and LCM Flotilla detachment. Gentlemen, be seated."

The stewards moved with practised efficiency and the meal went without a hitch.

"Port, gentlemen? And you may smoke."

Conversation turned, as always, to the war,

"What are we leaving behind?" asked Bridges.

Col. Jeffers, first in, with waxed moustache bristling, and his cheeks by now aglow with port, said, "Don't like leaving, be Gad, but the Air Force knocked Jerry out of the sky and made him think twice, then they made a hash of his invasion barges and troop concentrations. So much so that he turned his sights east, and invaded Russia. That should keep him busy for some time."

"Enough time for us to reorganise ourselves after Dunkirk," said Jimmy 'The One' (First Officer).

They all agreed. "Russia's too big; Hitler's bitten off more than he can chew. He's started his Barbarossa too late in the year; the winter will do for him. I believe that temperatures can fall below forty degrees below zero. Tanks and motorised transport won't be able to operate; both men and horses will be frozen to death," they all agreed in unison. The evening ended when the most junior officer present, Sub-Lieutenant Cordingly, as was the custom, proposed the Loyal Toast.

Marine Captain Alan Newsome MC, who had supervised the forming and training of No. 491 LCM Flotilla at Lympstone in Devon, had gathered around him what he hoped would be the experienced NCOs who would form the basis of a structured and well-balanced team. A thoroughly seasoned, experienced peacetime officer, decorated during the Norwegian campaign and mentioned at Crete, where he had escaped by the skin of his teeth, he was relishing his new assignment.

His sealed orders would have to await the arrival of his command and the sailing of the troopship.

THREE

FOUR DAYS BEFORE MY EIGHTEENTH BIRTHDAY AND just seven weeks after my medical a long brown envelope marked OHMS dropped through the letterbox, and the wondering and waiting were over.

"You are hereby directed to report," it read, "to the Royal Marine Infantry Training Centre at Lympstone, Devon, on the eighteenth of October. The attached warrant is valid for that date and your nearest railway station is Stoke."

The flat matter-of-fact directive brooked no argument and the conscription was in force from that date.

The local Co-op at Brown Edge where I worked and the Norton and Ball Green branches where I had relieved, cognizant of the fact that they would have to make up my wages for the duration of the war and to keep a job open for me when I returned, suddenly found a way to terminate my employment.

Such was their contribution to the war effort, but with most of my friends already in the Armed Forces, I, Jess Lambert, of Hill Top Farm, Clewlows Bank, Brown Edge, no longer saw my future in that kind of service industry, but I still viewed my call-up with apprehension.

Just enough time to say goodbye to my friends and close family and to travel to Birmingham to visit a girl I had recently met and whom I fully intended to marry, such was my certainty that no one else would ever do.

She herself knew nothing about it and would probably run a mile if she did.

I was gripped by excitement and fear of the unknown, but most of all by pride that I had been accepted into the Royal Marines, and like most of my generation I was full of the confidence born of ignorance that would be moulded into pride of achievement before I would be permitted to wear the coveted green beret that set the Corps apart and distinct from any other branch of the services.

We would be taught to survive in hostile conditions, to live off the land, to attack from the water, to move independently, to kill silently, to be completely

8

self-reliant, to be where the enemy least expected us, to harass and destroy, to enjoy a roving commission but with deadly directed purpose. The instructors would boast that the only thing they couldn't do to you in the Marines was to give you a baby, but if pressed they would even give that a good try.

The train journey from Stoke was a long and tedious affair; changing at Exeter for Lympstone seemed to sort us out into the weekly service intake that made up three squads each of ninety men.

Denny Green, who had picked up the train much further north and had struck up an acquaintance with me, leaned out of the carriage window, peering along the swaying curve of the train, eyes squinting to avoid the smoke and grit being belched out by a monster of an engine.

"Counted fourteen carriages," said Green. "Funny how the hiss of steam and the smell of smoke conjures up the excitement of going on holiday, but I don't suppose what we're in for will be much of a rest cure though."

"Whatever we're in for let's try to stick together and give each other moral support," I replied as we tumbled out onto the platform. "There seems to be about three hundred of us and they all seem as bewildered as we are."

Standing around in forlorn groups with our little cases and brown paper carrier bags we watched as the carriage doors were slammed shut, which effectively cut us off from our recent safe small world, and as the train pulled slowly out of the station we were enveloped in a cloud of smoke and steam.

As it slowly cleared, a uniformed sergeant appeared as if by magic on a pantomime set, but there the simile ended.

Our introduction to military life began as we were marshalled into some semblance of order and marched out of the station to board a fleet of canvas-sided trucks, to be ferried to the front entrance of the Marine Infantry Training Centre.

"Follow me!" shouted the sergeant as we dropped out of the back of the trucks, and in a long straggling file we entered the mess hall where we collected a substantial meal of bacon, dried egg, beans and fried bread. No civilian rations these, and if this was a sample of what was to come then it boded well for the future.

A tour of the camp, a midday meal followed by a welcoming speech and lecture from the CO in the main hall, which also doubled as a cinema, took up the rest of the afternoon.

The second day began with an 06:30 reveille, a strident bugle call from which there was no escape, then a general rush to the toilet blocks to take advantage of the limited amount of hot water to shower and shave.

After breakfast, which was just as good as our first meal on arrival, we queued up to receive the regulation issue of kit, each man filing past a high counter in the QM stores to have name and service numbers stamped on each piece of official issue.

"It's in your own interests to check to make sure that you receive your correct issue," shouted the sergeant. "Anything that is later found to be missing you will replace at your own expense."

Dressing ourselves later in the rough khaki battledress transformed each former civilian into some semblance of military anonymity. Packing up and sending our civvies back home effectively cut what remained of the dewy-eyed umbilical of youth and innocence.

Day three was taken up by dental inspections, minor treatments and inoculations against tetanus and smallpox which usually made the arms balloon up overnight. Standing in line to receive the shots in the arm dressed only in PT shorts and vest whilst a medical orderly came down the line to push a hypodermic needle into the arm muscle, leaving it dangling until the doctor followed him up to screw on the syringe to finish off the injection, smacked of Boer War butchery, with some of the biggest men keeling over whilst waiting their turn.

Sadistic NCOs, who mostly neglected to warn the new recruits to remove any tight clothing, which subsequently had to be cut to relieve the pressure, expressed neither concern nor sympathy, which prompted Jock Douglas, a dour Scot, to remark with some feeling to no one in particular, "I didn't expect anyone to kiss it better, but sympathy, that's another thing altogether. It appears the only place you are likely to find that is in the bloody dictionary, and you'll find it located between shit and syphilis."

No one was excused duty the following morning. "Exercise," we were told, "is the only way to relieve any pain."

Haircuts, a simple enough procedure normally, took on a larger-than-life importance when the barbers seemed to take a particular delight in demonstrating their skills and competitiveness with each other in cutting as near to the bone as they could to leave the shorn surface as polished as possible.

"Little bit off the top and leave the sideburns," mumbled Denny Green into a big blue cloth that had been quickly draped around his shoulders.

"Shampoo and massage sir?" queried the barber, and the clippers hummed as they wreaked their devastation.

The recruits looked on with apprehension as sideburns and hair were removed with careless efficiency, leaving the bewildered Geordie with hair clipped close to the regulation one inch above the ears, his pride and joy resting in forlorn heaps on his shoulders and lap.

"Anything else sir? Spray-lotion?"

"I'll tell you what," mumbled Denny Green. "Why don't I make you an appointment with a taxidermist?"

Not at all fazed, the hair assassin replied, "Leave the tips in the bowl at the end of the table, sir. We share them out at the end of the day." Turning, he shook the cloth all over Green. "NEXT!"

Robert Colman pencil-line moustaches and sideburns went in like a manner during the next two hours.

"I don't know why he held up a mirror behind me; we all look the bloody same," said Taffy Jones. "But I'd like to know who called that barber a prat... I would rather ask who called that prat a barber!"

Home for the next three months was a group of black-painted Nissen huts, lined each side with two-storey bunks, F Company left half. Twelve short weeks that would see pimply-faced youths transformed into a precision, well-drilled unit, fit and bursting with health and pride due to regular food, sleep, exercise and competitive training as a grounding for future specialisation and placement.

Mornings started with an 06:30 reveille followed by an hour's PE outside, whatever the weather, then a cold shower and shave, followed by a hot break-fast. Nothing was ever left on the plates except the pattern.

Nothing, however, could prepare us for an eight-mile-an-hour speed march over the Devonshire countryside in full fighting kit. Woollen socks and sweat-box leather shoes produced a fine crop of foot blisters which became a vicious problem no matter how you tried to ignore them or prematurely burst them.

Many different theories were voiced; washing them, using talcum powder or Vaseline. Nothing made any difference; all it needed for them to recover was rest, but this was not forthcoming.

Either by accident, design or indifference the training schedule got progressively more physical.

The assault course could well have been laid down for the Grand National but with more vindictive intent. It became something to be dreaded; every other day in rain, snow or sunshine gave it some familiarity whichever way they sent us around. The thing we seemed to remember was the water you fell in the last time or the seven-foot wall that got higher each circuit.

No one was excused unless you were dead; even then it was generally agreed that the instructors would make you carry the dead body over the obstacles.

Breath was something that nobody had to spare except for the ripe invectives that exploded after each mishap. To say that the instructors encouraged you was one way of putting it, the sergeant screaming that, "The Captain will take a bite out of your arse, and after him it's my turn."

Inter-squad boxing had its lighter moments; forget that your opponents were entirely random, and forget also that the ill-fitting gloves were not laced at the wrists.

All that the instructors wanted to see was all-out aggression. "The enemy won't be made-to-measure, get stuck in. Just knock seven bells out of each other for three minutes."

To win was fine, but to lose badly by covering up or without trying to win and you went into the ring again; no finesse, no ducking or weaving, just toe to toe slugging, the more blood the better.

It then seemed that the all-out aggression was channelled into a controlled unarmed combat.

The instructors coming at you with rifle and fixed bayonet yelling and screaming, then an absolute blur of movement practised over and over again until it became automatic and natural, enabling you to disarm your attacker and to turn his aggression to your advantage.

To kill with bare hands or feet when your enemy is down, stick your heel into his face and spin around on it; remember, if you let him get up he could kill you.

These lessons were driven home at every opportunity until we recruits wondered why we were issued with rifles and ammunition at all. The DPO rifles issued for arms drill without magazine or bolt were finally handed in and exchanged for their own 303 SMLE rifle and bayonet. The rifle range and butt at Honiton with targets for Bren and tommy guns tended to give a tunnel vision of an enemy. Pick them off before they know you are there, and then kill again before they can react, and again before they can come at you on equal terms. A good squad of perhaps twenty-five well-camouflaged men should account for nearly a hundred of the enemy before they are able to reply.

The instructors drew a graphic picture of a hunting pike following a line of swimming ducklings, taking the last one in line so as not to panic the rest. If you shoot the first the rest will go to cover and then you have a fight on your hands.

Orienteering and night map exercises were interesting; steer clear of local communities, live off the land for a week without stealing.

We didn't steal. We learned to accumulate, acquire and gather, which was stealing by any other name.

Vehicles which we hopefully tried to borrow had usually been disabled by the owners, either by removing the rotor arm, battery, starting handle, plugs or siphoning off the petrol. Local signposts had either been taken down or set up to point in any direction but the right one.

Back on the parade ground the precision and timing that had been ground in by repetitive drills and screaming instructors seemed suddenly to come together, steel tipped heels and rifle butts making but a single sound to the ears of nearly three-hundred marching men.

One instructor was heard to yell, "His Majesty has complete faith in me. He expects me to turn you into Marines. You've got as much military precision as a chimps' tea party." But there was no masking the pride in his voice at the subsequent passing out parade.

After we had passed in review order, we were dismissed from the parade ground to make our way back to our respective duties.

Passing the company office, we couldn't help noticing a group of NCOs going to see the CO. It later transpired that they were the active service personnel who had been drafted to our squads to take part in our subsequent training. A sergeant, two corporals and four lance jacks who would stay as part of our unit until the end of the hostilities.

The NCOs we had come to know during our initial training were camp fixtures and virtually all time-expired, so we shouldn't be seeing any more of them now that we were to move on for further training.

FOUR

ERGEANT JOHN THOMAS TIGHE, ROYAL MARINES, BETTER known amongst his fellows for obvious reasons as 'Dickie', lately of HMS *Recluse*, sat in the outer office of F Company RM Infantry Training Centre at Lympstone, Devon, waiting to report to the Officer Commanding, Captain Newsome.

Tighe was a big man, some six feet two inches in height, weatherbeaten, broad shouldered and tough. A man once seen to be remembered, about thirty-two years of age, fair hair, blue eyes, calm and steady with lightly etched crow's feet at the corners of the eyes, the product of good humour and of twelve years staring at shimmering and distant horizons.

The crow's feet at the moment were complemented by a frown, not of worry but of incomprehension at finding himself transferred from 'Big Ships' to what he considered the basement of his career. A career, the seeds of which had been sown at the tender age of six, losing both his parents in a freak road accident and leaving him to the tender mercies of 'Aunties' who passed him to and fro doing their 'Christian duty' with firmness but with little 'Christian love'.

A succession of schools had instilled him with the basics. This, coupled with a natural flair and determination to do well had taken him through the entrance examination to the local grammar school.

Two years later and with a school certificate in his pocket, he declined to take the Higher Certificate, which would have given him an automatic university entrance, and to the utter despair of his tutors and the "Told you so" tuts of his nearest kin he had packed his bags and left home.

Years later and in retrospect, he considered it the best move he had ever made, joining the Marines as a boy soldier. The service had become his family and given him that feeling of belonging that had been sadly lacking in his more formative years. With a more stable and settled home environment during his

14

early youth he would certainly have pursued his academic studies to one of the universities, but this would have required the guidance and parental stability that had been denied to him.

The comradeship and esprit de corps that flourishes in the Royal Marines and which he enjoyed has its roots in history; a sentiment that it is more than pride of regiment alone, for it is the human bond that unites a scattered brotherhood.

In spite of many and varied commitments, his normal function had always remained constant together with that of his comrades. He was a soldier who went by the sea and returned by the sea, whether ashore or afloat, whether he had joined for continuous service or hostilities, only he had been trained for amphibious warfare.

Their proud boast was that they were the first to land and the last to leave.

Now with sixteen years of training and service behind him and until recently in charge of Y turrets gun crew and its sixteen-inch guns, this transfer to Admiral Lord Louis Mountbatten's latest brainchild 'Combined Operations' was both bewildering and challenging.

However, his whole appearance exuded confidence and capability, and the feeling of superiority of a career NCO over these hostilities-only conscripts, culled from shops and factories and every other walk of life.

He didn't see himself as a wet nurse but his insight was sufficient to suggest that this war was not a regular's war any more, but was going to need the help of every mother's son before it was over. Being foremost a product of naval discipline, which meant above all the acceptance of the job in hand together with the prevailing circumstances, only in the mildest way would he indicate that this was not what he expected or was used to.

The sea had fascinated him as a child, and for him it was eternal. It would always draw him to her; he realised that it could be fatally attractive but any time that he spent away from her he considered wasted. He loved her in all her moods and treated her like the demanding mistress she was, unpredictable, moody and sullen, subject to tantrums and totally unfathomable, but like the love of a man for his mistress he could not do without her.

FIVE

ORPORAL GREG WINTERS, WITH SIX YEARS' PEACETIME service behind him and recently wounded on Crete, had been evacuated and subsequently spent two months in hospital convalescing. Upon his discharge, he had been separated from his Commando and transferred to 'Combined Operations' – whatever that meant. With the transfer had come another stripe, which when sewn below his lance jack's hook looked decidedly pristine. The few extra shillings that accompanied the promotion were particularly welcome as he now had a new wife to support. Leaning back deeply into an easy chair, he thumbed idly through a Zane Grey book he had picked up in the dining room of a dingy bedsit in Exmouth. Seated beside him on the arm of the chair was a pretty girl of about thirty years of age, his wife, married for only a few short weeks and who had travelled down from the Midlands to be together for his short weekend pass. This was the picture he would always carry with him wherever he went; his sweet Jane, glancing shyly at him and blushing quite furiously at the newness of it all.

"Do you know where you'll be going, Greg?" she murmured, catching his arm and pressing herself to him.

"No I don't, dear. I suppose that someone in the Admiralty does though, but in their infinite wisdom they never confide in me."

"Do you think it will be a long war?" Not waiting for an answer she continued as though she had been rehearsing it. "If it goes on for simply ages I was thinking I might as well move in with Mother. I'll take a few things with me to tide me over and shut up the house. I can still get to work from Mom's and at least I shall have someone to talk to. What do you think dear?"

Makes a lot of sense, he thought, but the idea took root in his mind, and due to the relationship he had with his mother-in-law it almost ruined their weekend. She was recently widowed, bitter and quarrelsome, not liking him at all.

16

"Could have done better for herself," she confided to her neighbours. "But who am I to interfere?"

Greg, however, tended to be quite philosophical about it all, realising how fortunate he was. However hard he tried, she seemed to begrudge them any small happiness they could find in each other; perhaps no one was good enough for her daughter.

Finding a small house about half a mile away had been the saving of their sanity, because her mother with her dicky heart could only visit when collected. She couldn't see that her sudden turns and convenient illnesses were counter-productive and tended to alienate those affections she strove to retain.

"I don't see why not, Jane; be company for both of you. It might also be worth considering renting out our place for the duration. Besides it will give you a little bit more income which is always very welcome."

He felt relieved that the discussion was closed, but remembered the row they had when the old lady had taken it upon herself to change the furniture around in their small lounge: "Mother didn't mean anything by it; she thought it would be more convenient this way."

Perhaps he was making a mountain out of a molehill, but better to nip things in the bud in the beginning. Calling it a bloody cheek he had promptly placed it back again.

"If she moves it again I'll nail it down. You really should try to be a little more assertive, dear. I know it's hard to break the habit of a lifetime and that you try to please everyone by taking the line of least resistance, but if you're seen as a soft touch people will try to walk all over you."

Jane always pandered to her mother and her dicky heart, although Greg secretly believed that there was nothing wrong with her, and that she used it as an excuse to get her own way.

Her husband Bill, a likeable and friendly fellow who Greg got along with like a house on fire, was after thirty odd years of married life inoffensive to the point of being docile, not being allowed to tie his own shoelaces, completely robbed of all his self-confidence.

"Doesn't matter, Greg," he once confided. "If it makes her happy let her get on with it. It saves any arguments and I'm sure she does it with love from her point of view."

The sad part of it all was that a few short weeks later he had to die to prove he was an individual. No one believed he was ill until it was too late. He went without demur, without asking his wife's permission, and with a half-smile on his lips, knowing that in the manner of his parting the last word was between himself and his God.

After the funeral the mourners were given a small glass of sherry, for which she scolded Greg, and unable to contain himself any longer over her narrow-minded interpretation of Methodism he heard himself saying, "Bill was not allowed to take an intoxicating drink throughout his married life but I would ask you to consider, Mother-in-law, it is not that which goes down the throat that damns the soul, but that which comes up over the tongue."

Yes, it would be better if she moved in with her mother, and that is how it was left.

Six

For those men not on guard duty or work detail after 18:00 hours, the chance to escape from the camp for liberty ashore for a few short hours tended to relieve the monotony. Bob Rogers and Taffy Jones took advantage of this four-hour break, catching the liberty boat outside the camp gates for it to drop them off in the centre of Exmouth.

Making their way to the Crown Pub they sat together at the bar sipping scrumpy, a rough cider brew that would strip paint from the side of a ship, and peering through the smoke haze at a couple of grim-faced tarts who had managed to attach themselves.

"Should we give them the order of the boot, mate?" Bob asked as they fought their way to the bar, screwing up his face at the thought of what might lie ahead.

Taffy made a momentous decision. "Seems a shame to waste an opportunity. When they've got all their clothes off and you've turned off the lights you couldn't tell the difference between them and the Duchess of Lympstone, except that the Duchess would make you do all the work."

The room was hot, noisy and packed with service personnel all pushing and shoving at the bar in their eagerness to be served. Those fortunate enough to be standing there refused all entreaties to move away when they had been served, fearful of not being able to order again.

The potency of the scrumpy to those who were unaccustomed to it would quickly become apparent when they stepped outside at the end of the evening. The beer regulars were disdainful of this apple juice, as they called it, and the locals smiled knowingly to each other as they discussed in their broad Devonshire accents the mother and father of all headaches that the servicemen were laying up for themselves.

Suddenly the bar went silent as the landlord switched the wireless on. "This is the Home and Forces programme," the announcer said. "Here is the news and this is Alvar Liddell reading it. Here are tonight's headlines. Japan has carried out an unprovoked attack on the Hawaiian naval base at Pearl Harbour. No declaration of war was made and four major warships have been destroyed and a further four badly damaged. The death toll is reported to be in excess of 2,300."

The silence in the room was suddenly interrupted by everyone talking at once, and the general consensus was: "Now the Yanks will come in. Now we won't be standing alone."

The room went quiet again as the announcer continued with his grim bulletin. "Two of Britain's newest and finest ships, the battleship *Prince of Wales* and the battle cruiser *Repulse* are confirmed sunk in the Gulf of Thailand by Japanese torpedo bombers called up from their base near Saigon."

The questions went around the room again. "Where the hell were the carrier escorts?"

It was to be learned much later that the carrier *Indomitable* had been sent as escort but had struck a reef off Jamaica and had been sent to the Norfolk naval base in Virginia for repairs.

"Sod's law," said Taffy when the wireless had been turned off. "The enemy will always kick you up the rear orifice when you least expect it! Anyway, back to the matter in hand," he added when Bob had fought his way back from the bar with four pints of Scrumpy. "What are we going to do about the couple of dogs we've landed ourselves with?"

"Don't worry, matey," came back the reply. "A standing p----'s got no conscience."

Both girls had seen better days and their skirts and blouses appeared to be a couple of sizes too small, imprisoning flesh that seemed to have a mind of its own and was doing its best to overflow and escape, all the time being forced into unnatural contours by the imprisoning clothes.

"One thing's for sure," mumbled Taff. "I'm glad we got an issue before we left camp; there's no way I'm going in there without an overcoat even if it's like having a bath with your shirt and pants on. I don't fancy visiting the sickbay on a regular basis for the next six months."

"What part of the country do you come from?" ventured the redhead, looking straight at Taff.

"Wales," he replied, trying to be sociable, and because of the obvious reason they were together he felt decidedly embarrassed.

"That's a long way. I've never been there." Her simulated Welsh accent prompted him mentally to note that if he got lumbered with this one he would put a bag over her head. Her friend, meanwhile, had been trying to interest Bob Rogers. Crossing and uncrossing her legs, which had been painted with gravy browning because of the shortage of silk stockings, and primly trying to pull down her short skirt which she somehow contrived to assist in riding up again, showing what she obviously thought was a provocative flash of unpainted white thigh.

"I bet you boys have girls back home," said Redhead, still pathetically trying to engineer some kind of dialogue.

"Oh hundreds, got 'em queuing up."

Suddenly making up their minds, both men jumped up and drained their glasses as if spurred by the thought of the approach of 23:59 hours, when their liberty pass expired.

The crowd standing around waiting for their table started to jockey for their seats as they began to push their way outside.

Once outside the two girls linked arms and with their heads bent against the driving rain pushed on at a furious pace.

"What's the rush?" said Taffy into his cupped hands as he tried to light a fag.

"I don't think it's so much eagerness or lust but time is money, and they've probably seen another couple of clients. Anyway, don't forget about Einstein's theory of relativity which states, 'What goes up must keep going up!'"

"Redhead says she has a birthday in a couple of days. What birth sign does that put her under?"

"Well, it certainly isn't Virgo," laughed Bob. "Neither is it 'No trespassing'."

Signing back into camp just before midnight Taffy muttered, "Was it all worth it? I've dipped my wick in some funny places in my time, but nothing like tonight's episode. If that's all there is to it I think I'm going to become a monk."

"Well, what else do you expect for ten bob?"

"Not a lot, I suppose, but for half a week's wages..." and the rest of his sentence trailed off. "Perhaps it would have been better if the gravy browning hadn't started to run with the rain."

"Yeah," his mate smiled, "but wasn't she beautiful when you turned off the lights?"

"Ravishing," said Taff. "Bloody ravishing."

After three months' basic training the powers that be considered that we were sufficiently presentable and of a high enough military bearing to reflect honour on the service, and we were allowed seven days' leave.

Jock Douglas, who had no home to go to, had been invited to spend his leave with Taffy Jones, and together they made their way to the Railway Station, only to discover that they had two hours to wait, providing the trains were running on time, which they seldom were due to the air raids and lack of rolling stock.

They sat on their upturned cases beneath a large propaganda poster which stared down at them, screaming its message in six-inch capital letters:

IS YOUR JOURNEY REALLY NECESSARY?

When the train arrived, three hours late and crowded, there was standing room only with the corridors packed from end to end with servicemen and women sitting on kit bags and suitcases. Jock and Taffy pushed their way through unceremoniously, apologizing, intent only on getting on board.

"Changing at Exeter, I suppose," said Jock, "so I guess we go through this all over again, unless it starts empty."

Which it did, but first they had to change platforms, up and over the bridge, at breakneck speed, to find the connection slowly pulling away.

Seeing them coming, some kind soul held open the carriage door, and throwing their suitcases in ahead of them to waiting arms they followed them in and sank down onto a seat. With thanks all around they pulled their berets over their eyes, and quite oblivious to their surroundings, like servicemen the world over, took advantage of the opportunity to sleep.

There was no restaurant car, no heating in the carriages in an effort to save precious coal, and the minimum of light, with one minute blue ceiling bulb that did nothing but add to the feeling of austerity.

The noisy click-clack continued through blacked-out and anonymous country stations (anonymous because the nameplates had been removed to confuse a would-be invader). Finally, after standing outside the main station waiting for the track to be repaired and the results of the latest air raid to be cleaned up, there was the noisy drawing alongside the crowded platform and the fight through a sea of bodies anxious not to be left behind when the train departed.

Standing outside the station, Jock Douglas and Taffy Jones pondered their next move, thinking what on earth could be more desolate than an empty platform at four o'clock in the morning with the rain coming down like stair rods.

The only noise they heard was the sound of the miners' clogs as they made their way to the pit for the early shift and the clink of the milk bottles being delivered to the rows of terraced houses that seemed to stretch and curve their way forever up the steep cobbled streets.

"Buses don't start 'till six o'clock so we might as well start walking. It's only about five miles and we couldn't get much wetter," said Taffy as he shook the rain off his cap.

Some time later and wet through, they stood in front of a neat, well cared-for house.

"For God's sake don't stand on the doorstep; it's Mam's pride and joy. She spends more time whitening that blasted thing than making her face up."

Jock, observing it in all its pristine glory, began to wonder what he had let himself in for, and it was all he could do to stop himself from running away.

"Mam's a good sort; you'll like her," said Taff, banging on the front door, which he kept up until the bedroom sash shot up and a grey head decorated in curlers leaned out to call, "Who's there, look you?"

"It's me, Mam," said Taff.

"Now there's lovely," she beamed. "Wait until I make myself decent and I'll be down to let you in." Almost in the same breath she continued, "Dad, get up and light the fire and call our Mary. Our boy's home."

Some time later after the introductions had been made, they were sitting down in a spotless kitchen to a cup of tea with Mam presiding over the table, resplendent in her new dressing-gown, with her face beaming with pleasure, but scolding them for not giving her some warning of their arrival.

"Fancy catching me like this."

"Couldn't help it, Mam. It all happened at once; gave us no warning, no time to let anyone know. Anyway I told Jock you would be pleased to see us."

Meanwhile Jock was admiring Dad's dexterity in peeling and re-rolling his tin of miscellaneous fag ends when he invited him to help himself from a tin of fifty Senior Service. Dad's eyes popped and his grin spread from ear to ear, as if he'd won the pools.

"Don't make yourself bad," said Mom. "He tries to make a packet of ten last him all the week. What are they? Passing Cloud, Lucky Strike, Camel, Turkish; it sometimes smells like a harem when he lights up."

"Lucky to get any at all, I suppose, and they're all under the counter too. I sometimes think that there is more under the counter than on the shelves, although I occasionally get a packet of Woodbines if I take the shopkeeper some vegetables from the allotment."

"Where's Mary got to, I wonder?" smiled Taff, looking sideways at Jock. "I suppose she's putting on her war paint specially for you." Jock, for some reason, felt himself starting to blush and feel distinctly uncomfortable.

The lino on the stairs did little to conceal the approach of Mary, who undid the stair door and stepped into the tiny kitchen, and for a brief moment stood framed in the doorway looking around.

"Let me introduce you," said her brother.

"No need to. You must be Jock that I've heard so much about." Mary offered Jock a slim cool hand. Standing up abruptly he took it, and in his haste knocked his chair over backwards.

Completely tongue-tied, he finally managed to blurt out something that he hoped was intelligent. Picking up his chair he sat down heavily and looked away, completely confused.

Gazing at her surreptitiously when he thought she wasn't looking, he saw a picture that completely captivated him: a heart-shaped face, surrounded by a halo of natural blonde hair, and a figure like Venus.

Later, when they had returned to camp and were unpacking Jock, in a more quiet mood and unusually studious for him, said to his mate, "That was a grand leave, Taff. I shall have to write to your parents and thank them again, but why on earth didn't you warn me that you had a sister like that?"

"Oh, she's all right, I suppose," Taffy answered, but there was no mistaking the pride in his voice. "Anyway, why do you think I took you home? I'm glad you and Mary hit it off; I wouldn't mind you for a brother."

What a leave, Jock thought, *and she's promised to write to me*. He continued to walk on air for weeks.

This short taste of family life suddenly brought home to him what he had missed in all his formative years.

He never knew his parents. His mother had put him into care shortly after he had been born. Growing up in the hungry Thirties with unemployment rife, particularly in The Gorbals, meant that even schooling was a hit-and-miss affair.

Any education he absorbed, sadly, was despite the school, and not attributable to it. He couldn't wait until he was sixteen. Then he made a beeline to the recruiting office and joined the Marines as a boy solider, and like many a lad in his position, they educated him, clothed and fed him regularly. In short, they enabled him to achieve his potential and he regarded the Marines as his home.

Another vista had opened up when Taffy Jones had invited him to his home and the future suddenly looked rosy, particularly as his romantic interest was aroused and reciprocated by Taffy's sister. He felt that all his birthdays and Christmases had come at once.

Snaps he had taken with a Box Brownie, when they were developed, those glossy flat squares, were all that remained of the laughter and delight of those few sunlit days. Jock Douglas put them into his wallet. Like the pressing of some lovely flower between the pages of a heavy book, it was the capturing of memories that possibly would have to last him until after the war.

Back in camp they were on the move again, to Dalditch in Devon, just a few short miles away, to be segregated into groups for training as coxswains, engineers and signallers. The latter were moved on again to the Signals Holding Company in Trecwyn, Pembrokeshire, and then on to Saundersfoot, there to be taught Morse code in all its forms, wireless telegraphy, Aldis lamp, semaphore and halyard signalling until they became a second language.

Months later they were to come together again in Strachur, Scotland, when they had graduated into their specialities. They were now welded into a completely independent fighting unit and fully integrated into Lord Mountbatten's Combined Operations.

The only question was now one of waiting, and rumour had the target as Europe; it had to be Europe. The cooks, as usual, had indisputable information, and even the batmen had seen it in writing.

Strachur also became the base for the coxswains to polish up their skills in handling the LCAs and LCMs on Loch Fyne.

Beach landings were practised until they could do them in the dark, and they often did. A coxswain guilty of broaching his assault craft suddenly became fatherless if he unloaded his men too far from the beach, forcing them to wade ashore in chest-high freezing water.

The one thing above all else that made life tolerable was the food. After a day out in the middle of the loch in November, or a 6:00 PE run up the side of a mountain in ice and snow, hot food was a must, and, credit to the cooks, it was always hot and plentiful. Unimaginative, but plentiful.

SEVEN

A T THE END OF THIS TRAINING THEY were sent on embarkation leave and dispersed to all points on the compass for ten days, all except Corporal 'Tinker' Taylor, whose home in Plymouth had been destroyed in heavy German raids.

A whole street had gone and he had no close family left. This was a period in history when aunts, uncles, cousins, nieces and nephews all lived within a stone's throw of each other and were close family units. All went to the same school, worked in the same factory, and now sadly had all died together.

Daisy Green, who knew something of his history, invited Taylor to visit him on his leave to Birmingham.

The train journey to the Midlands was a stop-start affair, with signal failures, unexploded bombs on the sidings and a shortage of rolling stock, and finally a wait outside Snow Hill Station for the fires to be put out during an ongoing raid on the City Centre.

Piling out of the train and walking down the track to the platform, they were advised to go to the shelters until the All Clear, but they decided to try to make their way home to Tyseley.

Leaving the station, they emerged into Colmore Row and made their way down Corporation Street and into Bull Street. The buses had stopped running out of the terminus at Carr's Lane; in fact, it had been closed off.

Fires were out of control in the High Street and New Street, a bomb had taken out the front of H. Samuels the Jewellers, and the road was scattered with rings and jewellery. So fierce were the fires that the tar melting on the roads was a moving black mass.

A landmine had wiped out the Malt Shovel Pub and the Co-op was bombed and ablaze. The Bull Ring Market Hall was gutted. Stonehouse Lane Police Station had been hit and an inspector and six officers killed.

The front of Greys Stores had been ripped out, and making their way down the High Street through Deritend they noticed that the valuable stained-glass windows had been taken out of St. Martin's Church, crated up and placed in the shelter on one side of the church. Fortunately, the bombs had fallen on the other side.

Continuing on their way towards Tyseley, they had to shelter in the doorways to avoid the shrapnel when they heard the bombs falling. Patrolling ARP wardens pulled them up and questioned their sanity, but when they mentioned embarkation leave they let them continue. They found that the Prince of Wales Theatre was destroyed and incendiaries had completely burned out Marshall and Snellgroves Store.

The Carlton Cinema was also a casualty. It had virtually disappeared. A bomb had fallen in front of the screen, killing nineteen people. They were found, still sitting bolt upright in their seats and totally unmarked, apparently killed by the blast that had burst their lungs.

Making their way through The Greet, Daisy and Tinker discovered that the BSA had taken a direct hit and the upper floors had collapsed, taking the heavy machinery down into the cellars. No rescue was deemed possible and the site was later to be concreted over to form a dedicated war grave.

After turning into Knights Road past the ack-ack gun on the island, they took shelter as a stick of bombs were released, finding targets in the Klaxon and the Abbington King Dick, but obviously seeking the Tyseley Railway Yard or Bordeseley Green Marshalling Yard.

"One thing's for sure, Daisy. There's no shortage of excitement going home on leave with you. We should be in less danger on the front line."

Finding nothing of his home, Daisy made his way to the wardens' post, a brick-built shelter with a concrete top. A number of men were playing cards. As Daisy and Tinker ducked under the screened doorway one of the younger ones looked up and said, "Look out everyone, the Marines have landed."

The oldest one said, "Just in time for a brew. Always a pleasure to see the Marines."

"Family of Green?" asked Daisy. "Numbers 16, 18 and 20 gone... only rubble."

The wardens looked at each other, and after a long embarrassed silence the oldest one, who took it upon himself to be their spokesman, said, "Green, Number. 16, family of three; Parsons, Number 18 family of two; and Number 20, mother, father and four children. We're very sorry, mate, we did all we could but there was nothing to find. It was a landmine. We saw it come down; it seemed to hang forever on its parachute. They must all have been sheltering in the Anderson, but that went as well… It only happened two nights ago, so next of kin wouldn't have been notified. The Town Hall has all the details. If there is anything we can do… They can't have known anything, Mr Green. It was all over in seconds. They couldn't have suffered."

Outside the clouds had blown away and the sun had come out. Men were clambering over the dusty, smouldering rubble. A deadly silence seemed to hang over everything, and for Daisy Green it was all happening in slow motion, to someone else.

"It doesn't make any kind of sense," said Daisy quietly.

"You come home on leave, feeling glad to be home, the family you had come to see are not around any more, not even a grave to mourn over; it doesn't make sense at all," he repeated, shaking his head in an effort to take it all in. "No bloody sense at all."

Like everyone who had been hurt, he looked around for someone to blame. "The Germans, the bloody Germans. I hope we get sent over there. There is a debt to be paid, in blood. I'm glad I came though, to see for myself. I couldn't have coped if I had been told by some official letter, some soulless bloody missive."

Tinker, aware of the enormity of his friend's loss, muttered, "I know it's no comfort, Daisy, but I went through the same thing a few weeks ago in Plymouth and it seems like fate that I should be with you in the same situation. It's still very raw with me too, and it does make you want to lash out. I know there's nothing I can do to ease your pain, but I'm here with you."

Daisy said very quietly, "I'm going to the church on the corner of Stockfield Road. That's where Mom always went."

"I'll come with you too; I haven't been able to go near a church since the events in Plymouth."

After a few quiet moments in church they were ready to leave when they were approached by someone whom they took to be the vicar, who hearing the reason for their visit started to trot out the usual platitudes. *Not his fault*, thought Daisy, but unable to contain the rawness of his feeling he said, "If this is how your Boss treats the good ones... according to you we should forgive the bastards who did it. Believe me, vicar, their time will come.

"Let's get out of here, Tinker, across the road to The Brit, Dad's old stomping ground. Got to wash the bloody taste out of my mouth. The last time I was here with Pops I had to take a two-pound jam jar because of the shortage of glasses. Perhaps his tankard is still behind the bar. At least the pub's still standing. Let's see if we can prise a pint out of the management. Normally you don't get served if you're not a regular."

They walked across the road and into the pub.

"Still the same old barman, I see," said Daisy. "Haven't called you up yet? What's on tap, then, for two thirsty Marines?"

"I can let you have a couple of pints of mild," the barman said, looking at their uniforms.

"Dad always called it 'arms and legs'."

"What the hell for?" asked Tinker, and suddenly he wished he hadn't.

"Because it's got no body; it's like gnat's piss, but at least it's wet."

"I thought it had been drunk before too, but I didn't like to say anything."

"Have these on the house, mate. Heard about your family. What can I say?"

"Not much, and thanks."

Making conversation the barman asked if they had heard about the train driver at Tyseley.

"What about him?"

"He's been recommended for some kind of medal for driving a train loaded with ammunition out to Earlswood, in the middle of the countryside, during the air raid. Probably saved the whole bloody community, let alone the station."

"Drink up and let's go, Tinker. Can't take any more of this gnat's piss. Can't offer you a billet, mate, but I am sure we can find somewhere to crash!"

"Thanks, barman."

"Good luck, lads."

"We might need it. Come on, Tinker, let's try the Sally Army."

The next day they made their way back to camp, a couple of days early, but what the hell.

Back in camp, they made ready to load kit bags and hammocks onto canvas-sided trucks for the short journey to Hunters Quay and a ferry ride to Gourock.

Everything seemed to be automatic. Nothing to plan, just go along with the flow. Their length of service had taught them to worry about what they could alter and accept what they couldn't.

The kit bags, not being required on the voyage, were unloaded from the trucks and placed onto large nets before being lifted by steam hoist into the hold of a darkened ship.

Meanwhile the Marines had paraded in a large dockside warehouse and were issued with snowshoes and skis, which were strapped onto each man's backpack. Now we were all sure of our destination the only speculation was how we were going to get into Europe.

The gangway of the darkened ship had been dimly illuminated and we made our way on board to pass through a canvas-screened door into a world of light and warmth, humming with generators and the overwhelming smell of freshly-baked bread permeating from the galley of the *Athlone Castle*.

EIGHT

THE AFT PARTY RATINGS UNDER THEIR LEADING hand had fallen in by the stern rails waiting for the officer to come to the quarterdeck.

The order was then given to take off the bow ropes and to single up to the stern wire, and to the leather-gauntleted mooring party to take off the wrappings.

The call went out to the hands on the jetty, "Cast off breast ropes and springs." Practised hands moved and the wires splashed into the water and were hauled on board.

Under the starboard helm the bows began to ease from the berth, the stern wire was slipped and the two accompanying tugs nosed the ship gently into the centre of the river.

In the dusky afterglow, the shore lights seemed to blink to challenge the rapidly approaching night that effectively hid what was probably the loveliest natural harbour in Britain.

The gale, far from easing, seemed to gain in ferocity. The crests of the waves began to topple, tumble, and roll over and the resulting spray began to affect visibility.

The captain and pilot, seeking what little protection the flying bridge afforded, stood duffel coated and gloved with shoulders bent, squinting to identify the various landmarks.

Our berth had been allocated and identified and the pilot announced that they were coming onto bearing. His job being done, the captain took over and called, "Stop engines." The telegraph rang shrilly, then once again for "Slow astern", and as we picked up stern-way the order to "Let go" was followed by the thunderous running out of the cable, and moments later the *Athlone Castle* was swinging gently in her allotted berth.

32

Below decks, only the gentle swaying of the hammocks above the mess tables betrayed the fact that we had slid from the docks. No bands, no fanfares of trumpets, no streamers or waving wives or sweethearts, just a silent slinking out of port at the dead of night.

A fitful, scudding moon revealed occasional glimpses of the Tail of the Bank merchant ship naval anchorage where scores of vessels were assembling.

On the near horizon, the bridge party recognised the silhouettes of a battleship, two flat-tops, and several cruisers, five or six destroyers and a score or so of minesweepers.

The other half of the convoy had been assembling in Liverpool Bay, beneath the comforting presence of the Liver Buildings with its ever-present twin Liver Birds.

The last feature to fade was the distinctive Blackpool Tower before, further north, the Bar Light Vessel, which marked the entrance to the Mersey.

The two halves of the convoy met and were chivvied into place by the destroyers that seemed to race around like nagging sheepdogs, snapping at the heels of their wayward charges before the Chicken Rock Light at the south tail of the Isle of Man and their progress into the open sea.

The rising wind whipped up the Irish Sea, which at the best of times was unpredictable, into a frenzy of vicious motion, making off-duty sleep virtually impossible.

The next day saw us making more marked progress, steaming northwest between Scotland and Northern Ireland.

Early evening gave us our last landfall, the sweeping hills of the Mull of Kintyre and the Isle of Islay further to the north.

Turning due westwards we headed for the open sea. Now that the watches had settled down to a monotony the signalling duties would be shared by the Marine Signallers contingent to make it a more acceptable two hours on and four hours off.

The gale blew itself out during the night, which encouraged a weak winter sun to come out, dispersing the early morning mist, and the biting edge of frost that had marked our night-time passage melted away, leaving a cheerful warmth and a general feeling of wellbeing.

The bridge watches became lonely and dreaded duties, and the zigzag routine set after joining the rest of the convoy became the only break in the tedium of a long night.

Twenty-five degree alteration to port with a run of ten minutes at sixteen knots, then two alterations of ten degrees to starboard and two following corrections to port for seven and five minutes consecutively, followed by a compensating sixty degree leg to starboard, covering in all approximately one and three quarter miles laterally to ships spaced at two thousand yards.

Without any stern lights showing on the vessel ahead, it would be too easy to close up without knowing it. Watchkeepers in the bows were therefore looking for a barrel being steamed from the stern of the ship ahead, the spray that it displaced being sufficient for them to keep station.

The twinkling Aldis lamps, the language of the night because of the imposed radio silence, prompted the duty officer to ask what it was all in aid of.

"Only chitchat, sir, greeting old friends, like pleased to have you along and how's the family," I replied.

Midnight saw a change of watch on the bridge, coinciding with a flurry of activity as the destroyers raced up the outside of the convoy responding to the sound of aircraft engines.

Two Foke-Wolf Condors had found the convoy as early as the third day out. The two long range maritime bombers could be seen circling overhead, the moon glinting on their reflective surfaces, well out of range of the ships' guns, pinpointing their positions and homing in U-boat packs on their vulnerable targets.

The duty officer sounded the alarm. "Captain to the bridge," he called on the voice pipe. "Sound Action Stations, gun crews close up, close all watertight doors."

The two aircraft broke away from each other and flew from opposite ends of the convoy down the centre line.

Their progress was marked by a huge fan of tracers, thrown up by every gunner as their guns came to bear.

How they survived was nothing short of miraculous, but survive they did, and at the end of their run they turned and dived and almost immediately released two bombs.

The first fell wide of any target, raising a huge spout of water, but the second one found its mark. It landed with a metallic clang on one of our convoy, and after the first mild explosion came a second one, a huge red and orange flash that illuminated the whole scene and for one unforgettable instant turned night into day.

The ship, whoever she was, had completely disappeared, there one moment and gone the next. The only evidence that she had ever existed were the sickening splashes of disintegrating metal raining back down into the sea.

"She must have been carrying ammo," said someone in the darkness of the bridge. "What a bloody way to go. The only saving grace is that they knew nothing about it."

Suddenly the moon went into hiding, as if ashamed to have provided the light to wreak such carnage.

There had been no trumpet call to arms with men facing the front to receive the enemy; they had been cheated of even the chance to defend themselves. During the next few weeks there would appear the usual brief communiqué in the newspapers:

"The Admiralty regrets to announce... Next of kin have been informed..."

It would effectively tear some families apart and touch others only briefly compared with the mayhem spreading around the whole mad world.

"It is as if a giant hand had wiped the characters from a blackboard," murmured a shocked DO as much to himself as anyone in particular. "Makes you realise what a tenuous hold on life we have."

"Quite the philosopher, aren't we?" replied Captain Bridges, visibly quite moved but noticing that no one had stopped to look for survivors except for the stern escorts, who would carry out a search pattern for a short time.

Nothing could have survived that blast, and any sadness that might have lingered and been brooded over was quickly dispelled by a second stroke of fate that gave an immediate answer to the activity of the escort destroyers dashing and shepherding their wayward charges like anxious sheepdogs.

Not a bomb this time, but a torpedo.

The U-boats called up by the attacking Condors had singled out a vulnerable target. We heard the torpedo strike the ship beyond ours, about three thousand yards away, and she stopped as if hit by a giant fist and had already begun to keel over at an insane angle.

She fell out of line like a scolded dog coming to heel, and as the rest of the convoy went slowly past little knots of men could be seen as they clung to the stern rails. The sea was on fire around them as the spilled oil caught and the swimming men fought the encircling flames only to be choked by the blanketing crust of oil.

The stricken ship seemed to stand on end like some pirouetting dancer, her screws exposed and still slowly revolving, poised ready to slide to its cold grave.

Men were losing their grip and falling into the topsy-turvy superstructure. Those who fell into the water were too close to swim away before she finally surrendered to the cold embrace of the endless ocean, sucking down with her any hopes of survival in her deadly downtow.

Bridges' first reaction was to stop and take any survivors on board, but the concern and pity was tempered by the thoughts of the safety of his own ship and the fifteen hundred or more men who were his sole responsibility, and the prospect of presenting a stationary target to any U-boat.

The problem was solved by an accompanying escort frigate, who launched two cutters and numerous floats. The men who were lucky enough to have survived the sinking could be seen scrambling on board and would subsequently be picked up by the stern escorts.

"Quite an eventful watch you had, I believe," said Sgt. Tighe to me as I came off duty.

"Sure did, Sarge, but I've never felt so bloody helpless not being able to hit back," I replied with some feeling.

The Bay of Biscay came and went and fully justified its reputation, the only satisfaction being that if it was rough for the ships it was a dammed sight worse for the U-boats, which possibly had to remain submerged to escape the worst of the weather.

Neutral Portugal passed on the port side with its shoreline blazing with lights some one hundred and twenty miles in length, illuminating the horizon, and after the blacked-out shores of the belligerents it seemed incongruous and vaguely disquieting, particularly as they were presenting a silhouette to any attacker from seaward.

Passage through the Straits of Gibraltar and into the Med saw most of the watchmen with bridge or deck duties sporting healthy suntans.

With Egypt beckoning, we passed through the Suez Canal, the Bitter Lakes, into the Red Sea, then finally into the Arabian Sea.

As the weather got progressively warmer, it provoked a lively discussion below decks and the question was posed, "What the hell do we do with the skis and snowshoes that were issued before boarding the ship?"

"That's top brass planning for you," someone commented. "They couldn't organise a bunk-up in a brothel. Like the committee who produced the camel, they were supposed to be designing the f-----g horse."

The shrill of the tannoy cut short any further discussion. "Now hear this. Now hear this. Starboard watch fall in. Special sea duty men close up."

The ship's routine had quickly been adapted to, which tended to dispel fears of the unknown, and of the ever-present submarine menace.

What if we had been hit by that torpedo and – fifteen hundred of us – consigned to the water or trapped below decks?

Once again the tannoy came to life, announcing: "Cooks to the galley and hands of the mess for grog."

"Come on!" shouted Cpl. Taylor, not backwards in coming forwards, who had been scrubbing his webbing straps. He picked up his eating irons and enamel mug. "Up Spirits!"

In time-honoured tradition everyone replied, "Stand Fast The Holy Ghost!" as they joined the end of the queue.

Nelson's Blood was a naval privilege, and holding their mugs out to the CPO each man was issued with a half-cup measure of grog that they had to drink on the spot and confirm by turning their mugs upside down as they walked away. Tradition also stipulated that if there was any surplus after every man had received his issue it was to be poured down the scuppers.

How some men managed to get rum down onto the mess deck was one of life's little mysteries. Debts were paid in rum, and strictly measured:

Two sippers = one Gulper.

Four Gulpers = one Tot.

Grog measurements were one part rum to three parts water.

Only watchkeepers and ranks of PO and above were allowed to receive their issue neat. This was probably the way it got down to the mess decks.

Dinner was collected by the duty cooks on each mess table, supplemented by doorstep wedges of bread, freshly baked and crisp.

"Bloody hell," said Bob Rogers. "I'm glad I broke my bread in two; I've just found two maggots!" Sure enough, the offending creatures were tipped out onto the mess table and scrutinised by curious eyes.

"They're dead," said Daisy Davies. "They couldn't possibly be alive having been through the ovens. Anyway, they're not maggots. I'm sure they are weevils!"

All eyes turned to him waiting for him to air his obvious knowledge about such matters, and he proclaimed loudly with an air of condescension, "Weevils, I'm sure of it, and the small one is the lesser of two Weevils."

It took some time for his remarks to sink in, but the ensuing laughter did not prevent the other bread being dissected and minutely examined.

The afternoon period began with the men parading in the flats carrying skis and snowshoes.

The end of the line saw them minus their winter gear and kitted out with full tropical equipment. Cotton khaki shorts, shirts, slacks, jungle greens, mosquito nets and bush hat, light underwear, virtually everything for an eastern theatre of war.

The exercise in subterfuge became all too apparent when it was pointed out that careless talk and fifth column around the dock areas could be disastrous and of paramount importance to an enemy if a destination could be ascertained.

The rest of the period was spent in scrubbing packs and webbing to remove the Blanco that successive training establishments had been unable to make up their minds about. Colours had varied from dark green to white.

These periods of 'make-do and mend' were popular and the opportunity to write home, even though the fact that we couldn't say where we were or where we were going limited what we could say.

Any breach would be subject to the censor's pen, and knowing that one's own officers were reading your letters and doing the censoring tended to make what you would like to say pretty restricting, being viewed by eyes other than those for which it was intended.

It must have been about one hundred miles from land when everyone became aware of the aroma of spices being carried on the warm evening breeze, and hours later we were standing in the sea lanes awaiting docking instructions.

We had arrived at Bombay, the Gateway to India.

NINE

BERTHING ARRANGEMENTS HAVING BEEN COMPLETED, THE TUGS nosed us alongside the Lion Docks, and curious troops crowded the rails to watch with interest as the local children dived into the water from the dockside to retrieve coins that had been tossed overboard. They were small-value coins: the anna, one sixteenth of a rupee, the rupee being about $1^s/6^d$ in English money, which had been converted before docking.

We were later to discover that many of the children around the dock area lived there, had no other homes, and existed only on what they could beg. This later proved to be a problem during a trip ashore, when we put our hands into our pockets in response to a small hand being held out towards us, and suddenly were surrounded by literally scores of street children, equally deserving and endearing.

Even with our poor pay, we quickly realized that we were princely in comparison, and the extreme poverty was brought home to us when we saw people fighting to reserve a place on the pavement to spread a meagre coconut mat to sleep on. What had reduced this beautiful people and country to this level? Was it a result of our country's rule, since the East India Trading company was formed, or perhaps too many people for a rural economy to support?

We had received lectures on board ship about the caste system to enable us to have some small understanding of the country, but nothing could prepare us for the reality.

However, war being a great leveller, no doubt the Indians themselves would sort it out after the cessation of hostilities.

The Indian Brahmin, we understood, were the socially or intellectually superior person. The Vaisya were the third of the four great Hindu castes, comprising merchants, agriculturalists, peasants, and labourers.

The Untouchables were said to defile members of a higher caste on contact, and the Unseeables were sections of people that didn't exist!

No difference really, from the English class system. The nobility, lawyers, teachers, doctors etc. And at the bottom of the heap, the unemployed and the unemployable, although the last two categories would undoubtedly find themselves in great demand in the event of war. To be trained to salute, and to march in step into the cannon's mouth.

No country could claim to be exempt from a class or caste structure, possibly the worst being celebrity or status measured by wealth.

The chance to debark from the *Athlone Castle*, our home for the last six weeks, to stretch our legs ashore and to sample some of the sights of Bombay together with the strange and new local dishes promised to be a pleasant experience.

In the meantime, however, we were marshalled into canvas-sided trucks for the drive to the naval transit camp situated about thirty miles or so into the country.

Leaving the capital behind we passed through small one-street communities where we could see various trades being practised in shop doorways and on the pavement.

Barbers were shaving customers out in the open and silver workers composing wonderful filigree work. Amidst all this, the sacred cows were wandering in and out of the shops quite naturally. People were the same the whole world over, with teashops, cafes, and workers in leather goods and ivory; beautiful work with the most basic of tools, but effective.

Finally we arrived at the transit camp, which was a joy.

The barracks, built with Indian labour, was typical – large, airy and clean. The construction was of split cane to allow maximum airflow, topped off with a corrugated iron roof, and sited on a raised concrete base. Each hut had been adopted by a char wallah, who would bring us a reveille-timed cup of tea together with hot water for shaving.

A punka wallah, too, had adopted each barrack room and was a must. He sat down on the floor all day and operated a large fan hanging from inside the rafters by a long cord attached to his big toe. It was certainly needed in the oppressive heat. With about forty marines occupying each room, it was decided to pay them forty rupees a week to split between them. This was unlooked for wealth and fights often broke out to obtain these regular jobs.

There was also a dhobi wallah, who would collect our soiled laundry and return it to us in about two days, washed, starched and ironed with creases like knives.

The clothes, however, wouldn't last too long with the kind of laundry practice meted out. They would soap them, whirl them around their heads to gather momentum and bash them against large stones by the river, swill them again and again in the river, and bash them until the water was out of them.

The Indian barbers allowed to work inside the camp set themselves up in an empty room and were a delight. Short back and sides, a shave followed by a hot towel and a head massage for the equivalent of 1^s/6^d, but no one availed themselves of the coconut oil pomade that the indigenous Indians made free with, although their black hair was luxuriant enough to recommend it.

When the camp had settled down to a routine we were allowed a liberty run into Bombay when off-duty time permitted.

The local people were open and friendly and seemed to go out of their way to be helpful. However we didn't fancy the local buses, with the locals riding packed inside and on top and clinging precariously to the window sills whilst standing on the running boards.

We grabbed a rickshaw and went sightseeing. It was usually left to the rickshaw drivers, who seemed to make a beeline for Seven Sisters Street, the red light district. Either the drivers got a bonus for supplying new clients or it was assumed that natural desires would rear their heads, so to speak.

The houses were on both sides of the street and the ladies displayed their charms quite openly in windows and doorways, coquettishly and invitingly. There, pimps and minders eager to exploit the potential new source of wealth gathered around the rickshaws extolling their clients' charms. "Very good jig-jig, Johnny, short time five rupees, all night long time ten rupees." At 1^s/6^d per rupee it seemed quite a bargain if you didn't consider the risks, which were the same the whole world over no matter where you went.

Not willing to risk the fare on offer we decided to go to the pictures. Reluctantly the rickshaws turned and made their way to the Victoria Terminus. *Molly and Me* was on at the Regal, and Ronald Colman was in a love drama, *Kismet*, at the Metro. Not fancying either we made our way to the nearest restaurant, and in common with all Jacks and Royals we had 'big-eats' and pints of Indian beer.

We returned to camp by 23:59 by courtesy of the liberty truck which picked us up at the Victoria Terminus. We were soon to realize that the pampering we were growing accustomed to was coming to an end; after all it was just a transit camp and no one promised it would last forever.

Packing up again, we were to board a train that was to take us to Cochin on the Malabar Coast.

This train journey was not to be confused with a holiday excursion back home; the carriages were quite basic, no glass in the windows, slatted wooden seats to allow for the circulation of air. The majority of the local passengers probably didn't pay for their fare and found precarious perches on the roof or stood on the running boards whilst clinging to the window frames. It was, after all, free travel and satisfying as long as you didn't fall off.

The toilet facilities were something else, like a shower tray with two raised platforms to accommodate your feet with an exit in the base where you could see the sleepers and tracks running by.

The latest transit camp provided the usual excellent facilities; plain, but clean and airy, which gave an excellent opportunity to send letters home and to allow letters from home to catch up with us. These make and mend periods allowed us to overhaul our clothes and equipment. Perhaps this was a planned means of acclimatization but it worked.

The local beaches were a dream; palm-fringed, golden sands and gentle rollers. Sunbathing was unnecessary as everyone was burnt a deep golden brown; everyone except the officers who wore their shirts, shorts and shady bush hats.

Perhaps sun exposure was only for the other ranks, although sunburn was a punishable offence as it could make you unfit for duty. Incidentally, an ENSA party sailing past the Cochin beach was reputed to have remarked on the troops' brown bodies, but questioned why we all wore white bathing trunks!

After two weeks of this idyllic existence we were packing again to board a ship of the Indian Navy, the SS *Nerosa*, to hug the coast, passing Ceylon, Madras, and Visagapatan to dock at Chittagong, the land gateway to Burma.

TEN

THE PORT OF CHITTAGONG WAS OUR LAST stop in India and as we debarked to face a two-hour drive in the canvas-sided trucks which literally set us down in the middle of a dry paddy field, Taffy Jones said, "It never ceases to amaze me where these trucks suddenly appear from. There always seems to be a never-ending supply."

"The mind boggles," laughed his oppo. "I suppose the little jeeps are their offspring. I'm trying to imagine their coupling!"

"Forget the coupling trucks and get them unloaded or you'll all be sleeping on the deck and out in the open, so move your arses! I want to see those eight-man tents up within the hour and the lot of you settled in!" barked Tighe.

Rows of tents sprung up and the bedrolls were spread. Suddenly the troops were at home. Wherever they laid their heads, they were at home.

We collected our packs and duffel bags, sorted our kit out, then, after the manner of all service personnel, began to wonder where our next meal was coming from.

The latter, however, was in the capable hands of an acting sergeant cook who set up his galley, which consisted of a row of three tents, set up side by side, and the cooking was done by a couple of volunteers, who incidentally gave a passable imitation of hungry gannets.

The open fire crackled beneath a flat steel tray on which a sea of eggs spluttered, and tins of boiled bacon and sausage were finished off by deep-frying. Mounds of fried bread were stacked at the side of the fire to keep warm and a dixie of baked beans bubbled gently on the fire, rubbing shoulders with a fanny of tea, sending an aroma to pervade the whole camp.

The duty sergeant stood with folded arms waiting for the rush to start. It wasn't long before a queue began to form; mess tins were filled with sausages, bacon, beans and eggs, topped off with fried bread. Each man's hands were fully occupied together with a mug full of hot tea as they returned to the camp area to eat.

The walk back to the tents, however, suddenly became a laughable and perilous journey. The kitehawks, birds that had been admired for their skill and aerobatics, now became rivals for the troops' food.

With a wingspan of some four feet they could remain virtually motionless on the warm thermals, the tips of their wing feathers searching like fingers for the slightest change in the upward rising air whilst scanning the ground for food.

Without preamble they suddenly folded their wings and plummeted to earth like an arrowhead, silently and with alarming speed. Approaching the walking unsuspecting victims from the rear, they swooped over their shoulders, and with a touch as delicate as any midwife, snatched the bacon, sausage, and fried bread from their unguarded mess tins with their claws and flew upwards, high into the air, to eat it on the wing at their leisure.

"Not bloody funny," I swore. "Never heard him coming, never felt a touch on my mess tin, never even disturbed a bloody bean, but he's nicked three parts of my soddin' breakfast."

"Should have warned you about the kitehawks," laughed the sergeant cook when the victims went back to the galley to see if there was any gash (leftovers) after everyone had been served.

"I think shitehawks describes them perfectly," I retorted, deliberately misquoting him.

The days that followed were full of sun, the only duty being arms maintenance. Weapons were stripped and oiled, knives honed, and surplus kit packed away. Even the watches set for the hours of darkness were tolerable duties, the temperatures falling to below freezing. Striding between the rows of tents muffled against the frost that suddenly came after the sun had gone down was a pleasant enough interlude.

Evening passes into Chittagong itself were a diversion for those not on duty. The liberty trucks usually dropped us outside the Chung King Restaurant. The driver probably had an arrangement with the owner; however, the food turned out to be about the best around. A good Chinese meal cost only two rupees eight annas (3ˢ/9ᵈ), and made a spicy change from camp food.

After one such meal, a group congregated outside wondering what to do next, when someone asked the question, "Anyone seen Bob? I'm sure he was here a few minutes ago."

"I think he's gone off to find a bag shanty. It seems he's discovered where he originated from and he's been trying to find his way back ever since. He'll turn up when the spirit's moved him, hopefully in time to catch the liberty truck back to camp."

Finding nothing else to do, and avoiding the pedlars and street urchins, we decided to go to the end of the road to await the transport back to camp, passing a crowd of local youths who congregated beneath the street lamps, surrounding themselves by splashes of red spit which stained the pavement as the result of betel leaf chewing. Apparently, this leaf was quite addictive and stained both the palate and teeth. We were later told that it was the leaf of the evergreen climbing plant, piper betel, and it was chewed together with the parings of the betel nut.

Returning to camp, there was something in the air. We all knew that; we had been in a state of readiness for the last few days. All our surplus kit and clothing had been sorted and packed into our sea bags and despatched to waiting transport ships ready for warehouse storage in India.

The troops were now down to their fighting packs and rations for fourteen days. Nothing had been left to chance, and any further waiting would see them over their peak and release that tension and anticipation that was part and parcel of a successful operation.

The light from the hissing pressure lamp that hung suspended from the ridge pole of the main tent that acted as both dining room and briefing room threw its feeble glow on the assembled officers and NCOs gathered together by the CO, Capt. Newsome.

Their attention, however, was drawn temporarily to a drama being enacted around the circle of light cast on the roof of the tent. Scores of moths attracted by the light were, one by one, meeting a sudden end. As they landed, hypnotised by the circle of light, there would be sudden rushes by geckos, lizards about four inches long. Running upside down on the canvas ceiling they would seize unfortunate insects and devour them. Only the wings were discarded and these would flutter down forlornly like whirling helicopter blades as if waving a sad goodbye to their bodies.

Unaware of what was happening to their fellows, the moths still came on. The appetites of the voracious geckos seemed infinite, and the maps spread out on the table below were littered by the debris from the aerial feast.

Standing up and shaking the maps Capt. Newsome said, "Gentlemen, the nightly entertainment is over. Let us put a different show on the road." Clearing his throat and looking around the assembled men he said, "Word has filtered down from above that we have been given the task of capturing the village of Kangaw. The Royal Marines of 3 Commando Brigade (1, 5, 42 and 44 Commando) together with troops of the Indian Army will accomplish this. At the same time and under cover of the attack I shall take a small force of men over the Arakan Yoma to destroy the storage facilities and production capabilities of the oilfields on the Irrawaddi."

This matter-of-fact statement had the effect of cloaking the enormity of the task to the listening men, making it seem not only feasible but desirable. The tension broke and the questions flew back and forth.

Capt. Newsome continued when the hubbub had died down. "I have already chosen the men to go along with me, and their names are..."

The listening men waited whilst the list of names was read out, and the disappointment of those not chosen caused Capt. Newsome to say, "Sorry, gentlemen, I consider that twenty is the correct number to accomplish this mission. It's either twenty or a brigade. If I've chosen correctly we won't need a brigade. If I haven't a few more won't make any difference at all. The most important element is surprise and we're more likely to achieve this with a smaller number, but I can assure you that those not going will have their hands full with Kangaw, so don't think you are missing anything. On the contrary you are probably getting the rough end of the deal."

His audience drifted away in groups of two or three some time later, the majority to seek late beds, but those chosen to discuss far into the night the stores and equipment needed to sustain the operation to the oilfields.

The following day the landing craft, LCMs and LCAs, were ferried to the port of Chittagong and hoisted on board the transport ships preparatory to their departure to lie deep into the Bay of Bengal, between the port of Akyab and the island of Cheduba, ready to launch the attack on the village of Kangaw.

The main body of the Indian contingent was already on board and the Marines would be joining them the next day.

ELEVEN

LCM 654 NOSED GENTLY UP THE KALADAN River. Her twin diesel engines barely ticked over but her bow wave made the reeds and long grasses that lined the banks dance and sway in the arrow of her wake.

Stoker Bob Rogers sat between the gently purring monsters in the cramped engine room. Even sitting down he had barely six inches of headroom. With left and right hands hovering over the throttles, ready to reply to the telegraph from the cox, adrenalin pumping and sweat streaming from every pore due to the exertions of the last half hour, having run the gauntlet of the Japanese gunners who still controlled both banks at the mouth of the river.

Sergeant Tighe crouched in the armour-plated wheelhouse, peering through the observation slits and seeing nothing but the big bow ramp in front and the claustrophobic jungle crowding in on both sides.

Douglas and Green, the two acting deckhands, and myself, the signaller, who comprised the rest of the crew, were making ourselves small, flattened against the hot steel deck, sheltering behind the armour-plated freeboard of the craft.

We raised our heads occasionally between the fore and aft bollards to call out course adjustments to the cox, and took it in turns to unship the sounding pole to probe the river to avoid shelving sandbanks.

Suddenly the object of our trip upriver became apparent. The cacophony of bird and animal noises ceased as the air became alive with machine gun and small arms fire that poured in on us from both sides of the river.

"We've found the yellow sons of heaven," shouted Tighe. "Let's get the hell out of here!" The big twin diesels responded to full ahead port and full astern starboard, and the ungainly craft pirouetted in mid-channel and roared off downstream with the bullets dancing off her armour plating.

Four hours later, under cover of darkness and on a falling tide, we drifted silently past the Japanese defences at the mouth of the river and later tied up at the jetty at Akyab.

"Get some grub and I'll report in," said Tighe. Picking his way between the rows of tents, he found Capt. Newsome and Lt. Perry poring over maps in the main tent.

Looking up, the Captain said, "You found them, then?"

"In force, sir, perhaps platoon strength, both sides, about twenty-five miles upstream."

"Casualties?"

"No, sir."

"Well done, Sergeant. We'll try the Lemro entrance, going in just before first light. Get some sleep. 454 will be fuelled and ready by four thirty."

At four o'clock and with a rough awakening by the patrolling sentry we slipped the mooring lines from the LCM, moved silently away from the jetty, and took bearings for the Mybon estuary.

The short journey from Akyab was uneventful, and the rest of the crew, one at a time in the cramped engine room, were able to join stoker Rogers, who was lovingly caressing the big diesels with an oily rag, prompting Daisy Green to remark, "I reckon you think more about these engines than you do of your old woman. I hope you don't wipe her down with an oily rag!"

"Not likely," Rogers retorted. "These beauties respond to my slightest touch. Not like my old gal. I could stroke her arse all night and she'd still pretend to be asleep. She develops more headaches about half an hour before bedtime than any other person I know. I can look at the clock and think, any time now she'll ask me to get her an Aspro and a glass of water. She's the only person I know who can sleep balanced on the bed iron leaving me ninety per cent of the bed. I don't go to sleep exhausted or counting sheep; I count the curlers on the back of her head."

"So how long have you been married?" asked Daisy Green.

"Nearly seventeen years."

"Why the hell do you stick with her then?"

"Well I suppose it's somewhere to go on leave to. She's a good mother, and a damned good cook, and I'm away a lot, being a regular."

"How the hell did you get close enough to her to have kids?"

"She hasn't always been like that; it's only been the last fifteen years."

Daisy searched his face for any sign of tongue-in-cheek, found none, stubbed out his cigarette and came up from the engine room thoroughly disillusioned.

The Lemro River, running parallel to the Kaladan and perhaps ten miles further south, was the second phase in the Marines' probe to find the line of the Japanese escape route over the Arakan Yoma, a mountain range that followed the contours of the coastline and blocked the way to the Irrawaddi River and a free passage to Rangoon.

Taking full advantage of a rising tide, the darkened LCM floated silently into the mouth of the river and past the enemy's defences until we were far enough up the river for the engines to be started.

"Craft on the port bow," sang out Daisy Green moments later.

"Let it come on. It might be native. We don't want to attract too much attention. And keep your voice down," murmured Tighe.

Slowly the distance closed between the two craft and the Bren and tommy gun barrels were withdrawn as the situation unfolded.

"It's a bloody cow," laughed Daisy Green, releasing all the pent up tension.

"No, it's a water buffalo, I'm sure," said Bob Rogers, poking his head up from the engine room. Sure enough, floating upside down with its four legs pointing stiffly to the sky, and its head submerged at the rear acting as a crude rudder, the water buffalo, dead and badly distended by internal gases, was making its way to the sea.

Bets were taken as to how it would act if a small hole was punched into it at the rear, below the waterline. Would it put-put down the rivers like a motorboat, or if the hole was above the water would it act like a released balloon?

"That's pure methane in there. Some bird with a sharp beak or a hungry croc is going to get one hell of a shock if they try to take a bite," we all agreed.

We were still laughing when we came under small arms fire from both banks, and having once more achieved our objective we turned around and made our way towards the mouth of the river and the safety of the open sea.

Any chance of slipping out to sea unobserved in daylight or lying up until dark was virtually nil. The gun batteries would open up on us as soon as we were spotted.

We can only postpone the inevitable, thought Tighe, *but any indecision on the enemy's part could only be to our advantage*. With this in mind, we unshipped the sounding pole and lashed it vertically between the winch housing and the tripod jackstaff. Securing the green deck awning to the top, we draped it over the ramp and secured it to form a crude sail.

"I don't suppose it's going to fool anybody but it might give us a couple of hundred yards, and maybe they will think we're a native craft," said Tighe hopefully.

The waves and surf could be seen in the distance, and as they approached the escape route to the sea the shore batteries, not fooled for a moment, opened up on us. Towers of water erupted all around us, and it was at this point that Tighe decided to vacate the wheelhouse and con the boat by its engines. Joining the rest of the crew lying on the deck he called out adjustments to the engines' revs, conning the craft to the centre of the channel.

Vacating the wheelhouse, spontaneous though it was, undoubtedly saved his life. The next moment an accurate shot from the shore carried away the stern superstructure, steering helm and their makeshift sail.

The twin rudders, without the guidance of the helm, began to respond to a different law, probably Murphy's, suggesting that whatever could go wrong probably would, and the unequal battle with a racing tide started to take us slowly but surely towards the shore battery.

"Sod this for a game of soldiers," I shouted. "Come and join me, Daisy."

Together we crawled along the deck, and clinging to the torn metal lowered ourselves to stand on the twin rudder guards. The churning of the props at full throttle made the footholds precarious and treacherous.

"What shall I do if I lose my leg down here?" shouted Daisy above the roar of the engines.

"Don't worry," I shouted back, "I'll get you a crutch and a bloody parrot."

Standing with one foot on the rudder guard-rail, we thrust the other down on top of the rudder, and our combined efforts gave some sanity to our headlong dash.

Later, out in the Bay of Bengal and out of sight of land, we were able to throttle down and take a more leisurely route to Akyab and the safety of the jetty.

The debriefing that followed allowed the enemy's lines of withdrawal to be plotted, and the part that Green and I had played was duly recognised and would probably be mentioned when dispatches were sent back, much to our embarrassment. Making our way back to our tents, Daisy Green couldn't resist saying, "The next time you want to play heroes, let me know in advance and I'll find some other way to lose my bloody foot."

TWELVE

AFTER NEARLY TWO AND A HALF YEARS of struggle and humiliation, which had culminated in the bombing of Calcutta by the Japanese from the air base at Akyab, the tide of war was finally beginning to turn.

Success had been achieved on the Arakan coast, the objective so nearly realized on two previous offensives. After the Mayu Peninsula had been cleared of the enemy, we mounted an amphibious assault on Akyab with its naval and air forces, only to find that the enemy had evacuated the day before.

The naval landing was made on the west coast, while the Indian division that had been operating on the Mayu Peninsula, ferried across from Foul Point. The island was found to be considerably damaged, with buildings and shipping destroyed, presumably by the Allied bombing.

As Akyab was ranked the third seaport in Burma it was considered a prize of some value, being situated around the corner of Akyab Island, and presenting straight frontage to the harbourage, which had water deep enough to take naval vessels up to cruiser size. It also boasted a certain number of quays and two landing piers along the waterfront. The island was separated from the mainland by a narrow waterway and the airfield could be used for attacks on the mainland of Burma.

When Ramree Island had been secured, and during the pause between operations, we were told to set up a temporary stage for a visiting ENSA party.

There must have been some 500 men sitting around the makeshift stage waiting for the entertainment to begin. It wasn't much of a show as shows go, but at least someone made the effort.

The only act was a cabaret singer, Patricia Burke, accompanied by an accordionist, but the show was appreciated and greeted with wolf whistles. To see a female in an evening dress in these surroundings was unreal and not a little unsettling.

A few days later, we had a visit from the Top Brass, Lord Louis himself, the 'White Knight', who arrived without any ceremony. We could only guess that this was for security reasons.

The informality of it took us all by surprise. Arriving by air and being picked up by jeep, his entourage stopped and the Earl stepped out and climbed onto the bonnet.

"Gather round," he called. No edge, no side, just one of the lads, and if that was what he intended, he succeeded.

He gave a pep talk about the conduct of the campaign and of the end being in sight. Whether this was seen as the beginning of the end or the end of the beginning one could merely conjecture, but the enthusiasm that the visit engendered could only be seen as beneficial. He certainly had that charisma that encouraged you to follow him.

Ramree Island had nothing to recommend it beyond its strategic advantages; it possessed a tremendous rainfall, very few inhabitants, virtually no cultivation, and a very bad malarial record.

We had quickly learned to cover up any exposed skin in the evenings because that was when the mosquitoes came out to dine on any exposed flesh. The wrists, forehead, and behind the ears were the first to be attacked and soon became swollen and puffy, marked with angry red spots.

We all seemed fitter; at least we had all lost weight, due to the continuous sweating. We never seemed to be able to get enough to drink. You couldn't trust the still water; that was where the mozzies would breed, and you could see the minute larvae wriggling around. It had to be boiled and treated with a sterilising tablet.

The island boasted only a small airfield but plenty of scope for extensions for making others. Its position with regard to Tangup on the mainland, with the latter's connecting roads to Prome on the Irrawaddi, opened up the opportunity to mount air attacks on the enemy-held positions. The island itself was only forty-five miles long, with the chief town Kyaukpyu at its northern end.

Cheduba Island, south of Ramree, became the next landing, increasing the Allies' hold and initiative.

The southern tip of Mybon Peninsula at Hunters Bay, some thirty-two miles from Akyab as the crow flies, was attacked with fire from machine guns and 75mm guns and was the first combined operation in Burma against the Japanese. After severe fighting, the enemy's positions were overrun and silenced by the Marine Commandos supported by the Sherman tanks of the Indian Cavalry Regiment.

The main attacking force destined to land at Kangaw had spent the night riding at anchor aboard the big transport ships some ten miles offshore.

Two hours before dawn we were awakened, and we breakfasted. Our personal equipment was checked and re-checked nervously. Cartridge belts, grenades and magazines were issued.

Helping each other into the heavy pack harnesses was a natural culmination of effort, and the relief that replaced the previous nervousness was evident as we troops lost ourselves in the various tasks.

Each man carried seventy-five rounds of ammunition together with four delay-fused mines. Australian slouch hats were worn at jaunty angles together with anti- malarial veils rolled onto the brims ready for lowering in the evening.

A typically equipped Marine would carry a tommy gun, *panga* (a long-bladed machete), revolver, razor-edged commando knife, a six-foot by two-foot waterproof groundsheet and a light woollen blanket, and would wear rubber-soled hockey boots for silent marching. For food we carried a mess tin, a water sterilization kit, and fourteen days' paratroop rations. These consisted of ten digestive biscuits, two ounces of cheese, two ounces of nuts and raisins, four ounces of dried dates, and a two-ounce chocolate bar, plus twenty cigarettes, two packs of matches, vitamin C tablets, powdered milk, tea, sugar, salt, and most important of all, sheets of toilet paper. Anything else would be supplied by Dakota drop, or we would have to live off the land.

Daily salt intake was of paramount importance because of the continuous sweating. The absence of salt would result in sudden collapse, fever and often, death. Early morning parades had always stressed the importance of salt and of using our two spoonfuls daily, together with anti-malarial mepacrine tablets.

Experience also taught us that when we were absorbing our full intake of salt our sweat-soaked shirts would dry with a coating of white dust upon them. Another test was to taste our own sweat.

Meanwhile the steam derricks were beginning to launch the LCMs, and the special davits to lower the LCAs were uncoupled as soon as they touched the water. The landing craft crews took their station on board – cox, engineer, signaller, and two deckhands. The craft were swung over the side and lowered to the loading decks to be secured below the scrambling nets.

The LCAs loaded three lines of men, the two outer rows sitting under the protection of the armoured freeboard, whilst the centre file crouched low on the centre deck.

The gaggle of craft had now begun to circle, setting themselves for the beach, the smaller craft taking station between the tank landing craft carrying the assault vehicles. We had some ten miles to go, and only sixty minutes to do it in before the dawn came up and the signal to depart was given.

Following in line ahead, we entered the mouth of the Theygan River on a rising tide and made our way along the corridor of mangroves that lined the *chaungs*, the tidal waterways that spread and criss-crossed the coastal plains like so many country lanes, but which were navigable only at high tide.

The enemy, expecting a frontal assault, was taken completely by surprise by the encircling movement from three separate points and was caught facing the wrong way.

The confusion was sufficient to allow the attackers time to obtain a landing and secure a footing on a prominent feature a little way from the beach, their first objective, known as Hill 170.

This still left them about half a mile from the village of Kangaw, their main objective. The importance that the Japanese attached to the village was soon evidenced by the vicious counter-attack they made on the British advances. Creating an escape route that gave them access to the winding coastal track, a tortuous hill path that wound its way up to An Pass over the Arakan Yoma, the mountain backbone of Burma, and from there down to the metalled roads and oilfields on the Irrawaddi.

Wave after wave of suicidal charges were made by the enemy, oblivious of the number of casualties. They pressed home their attack led by fanatical officers and NCOs waving their swords. The forward gun positions were overrun and the ferocious assault was only halted and turned on the lower slopes by blanket fire and a grenade attack.

The tenacity of the enemy from their entrenched positions was proving quite a stumbling block and it took two full days to capture the hill and a further week to take the village.

Only just in time did the British and Indian troops occupy the recently vacated enemy positions. The Japanese regrouped themselves and made a valiant effort regardless of losses to recapture the hill. In two days of severe fighting the enemy lost more than two thousand men. More than three hundred and fifty were counted on a piece of ground no bigger than a football pitch.

The lull that followed the attack was unreal, and suddenly on the third day there were no more Japanese in the area. During the night, the main force had cut a loop track around the village and slipped past. Suddenly there was no battle to fight. Ten thousand or so men and the tons of stores that had been put ashore were no longer needed, and the troops found themselves on the landing craft again pursuing the enemy, who were trying to escape from the small island to the mainland in small boats and anything that would float.

Challenged to stop, these frail sampans would invariably end up being rammed and the occupants dragged from the water and stowed resentful and terrified in the bow sections of the LCMs. They were poor specimens, completely dehydrated, and probably glad to be taken prisoner. Although they looked upon the latter as a disgrace they were happy enough at the prospect of food and water.

The British wondered, had the boot been on the other foot, what kind of treatment would they have received?

One Allied landing party of nearly three hundred and fifty men, attacking through the coastal mangrove swamps, were decimated by the natural inhabitants. The saltwater crocodile, reputed to be the most dangerous of its species, attacked in a feeding frenzy, and by morning, only twenty men were still alive. More than three hundred had been eaten alive.

Suddenly Sandaway and Gwa, coastal towns situated halfway down the peninsula towards Rangoon, which for years had been bracketed together and spoken of in the same breath as Marks and Spencer or *Romeo and Juliet*, were in our sights.

Names conjured up from storybooks and half-remembered pirate and spice tales, exotic names, redolent with the magic and mystique of the east, were openly talked about. Coco Islands, the Andamans, Nicobars and Indonesia, even Singapore, had begun to take on more flesh and were seen as a distant possibility.

Meanwhile a battalion of Gurkha parachutists had taken an enormous gamble and landed on Elephant Point at the mouth of the Rangoon River, killing thirty-six of the enemy and capturing one, this being the only opposition they met. At the same time a badly briefed Royal Air Force bombed the Gurkhas at Elephant Point and inflicted casualties.

The planes next attacked the jail, on the roof of which the prisoners had painted that the Japs had gone, and on their way back to base for good measure had machine-gunned a straggling column of our own men, prisoners held by the Japanese and abandoned in their haste to escape. The unfortunate brigadier leading the men was killed on the day he became a free man after three years of captivity and ill treatment.

Such were the vagaries of war, but all this was in the distant future, and in the meantime there was Sandaway and Gwa.

Thirteen

THE PERSONNEL LANDING CRAFT (LCP) THAT THE British intended to use on the first part of their journey were of flimsy construction, being plywood-clad, and afforded no protection even against small arms fire. The *chaungs* could flood to a depth of between ten to fifteen feet at high tide, and then drain at low water uncovering impassable mudflats inhabited only by mudskippers a species of fish equally at home on the land as in the water, and armies of fiddler crabs that emerged from the mud to feed after the receding waters.

Along the course of the *chaungs* the kingfishers and snipes wheeled and dived, whilst ever-present vultures soared high on the rising thermals, scanning the ground for whatever was on offer. These impartial undertakers of nature showed no preference for friend or foe and would descend and perch expectantly on the top branches of the trees in serried rows. Black and sombre, confident and efficient in their role to clear up after the tooth-and-claw brigade had taken their fill, their crops so full that, like a heavily laden bomber, they needed a longer runway to take off.

A cacophony of noise greeted them. The demented sounds of the hoolock gibbon and the eldritch howls of the hyenas and jackals could be recognized amidst the clamour and din.

The banks were lined with the twisted and gnarled roots of mangrove trees that were exposed at high water. This stinking labyrinth was also the home to a nightmare of creatures: crocodiles, leeches, water snakes, scorpions, mosquitoes, and a myriad of insects.

The only way through this maze was by boat, and only then at high tide. Misjudge the tide and the venture would be over before it had started.

We had a vision of ourselves sitting marooned on a mudflat waiting for the next high tide to float them off – that was dismissed by the distant noise of battle being fought for the village of Kangaw. The big central diesel engine roared into life as the throttle was pushed forward. The bows suddenly lifted as the screws dug deep into the dirty brown river and the resulting surge threw everyone temporarily off balance.

All outside sounds were drowned by the swell and vibrations. Like a cathedral organ, putting an end to all conversation and making ears ache and eyes close involuntarily against such an invasion of sound.

Throttling down some fifty minutes later, we turned in towards the bank where the falling tidal water was already beginning to manifest itself by the amount of exposed mud. The need to disembark safely was becoming urgent.

After pulling the craft into the dense scrub with the aid of a boat-hook we clambered out and unloaded the stores and equipment. The landing craft that for so long had been our home and transport was now surplus to requirements, and an embarrassment. Unable to send it back or camouflage it, it was decided to abandon it.

The seacocks were opened and it was set adrift. As the current took it away it began to take water on board and sink lower and lower, until with a rush of air from the ballast tanks it sank out of sight. Watching it finally disappear, our hearts sank with it, as it dawned on us we were now on our own. The last contact with some kind of security had gone.

"Like having your home repossessed and finding yourselves on the street," said Daisy Green.

"Well, don't wait for a removal van; pick up your gear. We're not waiting for a lift," said Tighe.

Following each other in single file into the forest was like stepping into a half-lit cinema, the dense canopy allowing only occasional glimpses of light like an usherette's torch. Although we were out of the direct sunlight the humidity and chill made us sweat profusely and our stumbling exertions only added to our discomfort.

We felt like intruders. Human feet didn't belong here. Time had passed this place by and meant nothing. It was neutral, gave no quarter; its attitude was death.

The sky above the canopy was livid, a merciless dome. The air had been breathed by millions of creatures and rejected as foul and unacceptable. Added to this our main aversion was crocodiles, creatures that had changed little, if anything, since prehistoric times, and that were without feeling of any description, with compassion and tenderness reserved exclusively for their own young. The way they carried the newly hatched offspring down to the water in their mouths was something that had to be seen to be believed. The natural aggression of the newborn as they emerged from the egg, nipping and biting, boded ill for some poor creature.

They were totally without fear. A sudden rush from a fifteen-foot reptile was virtually unstoppable. A body show wouldn't deter them; their hides were so thick a bullet would merely ricochet off. Only a direct hit between the eyes into the brain the size of an apple would kill, and this target was hard to hit when confronted by a gaping mouth more than three foot wide.

"I bet a hand grenade tossed into its cakehole would shut it up, although a mouthful never stops my mother-in-law," mused Greg Winters.

"Anyone would think you didn't like her," said Taffy Jones.

"No not much, but I wish she was here now; she'd be more than a match for these prehistoric bastards."

The going was now getting more difficult by the minute and it was only with the aid of our *pangas* that we were able to make any progress at all, taking it in turns to lead in half-hour stints.

No vantage point was high enough or clear enough to give us any idea of the forward trail, so our direction was entirely by compass and our aim was to cut the trail to take us to the An Pass.

Eighty miles as the crow flies would probably mean as much again by this tortuous route, but there was no other way to do it, and do it we must if we were to deny the retreating Japanese army a Dunkirk down the Irrawaddi and the metalled roads to Rangoon. The speed of their retreat meant that it had to be done within the next few days to be effective, to deny them vital fuel and transportation and, if possible, to force them to stand and fight.

Four hours later the vegetation began to thin to reveal the *chaung*, which had traced a tortuous loop following an easterly course. For the next two hours we had to be content to cut and follow a track parallel to it, knowing that despite our efforts we were getting further away from the track to the saddle pass across the Arakan Yoma. The necessity therefore to cross the *chaung* began to take on more urgency. The slack water period had passed and the water was now receding to the sea, soon to leave an impassable mud barrier. Caution and common sense, however, dictated that we should seek a more secure crossing, and a forward party was detailed to search for it.

This decision, obvious though it seemed, was to be tragically emphasized. You were never alone in the jungle. Somehow, somewhere, something was watching you, either sizing you up to be avoided or stalking you as its next meal.

The Marines settled down to await the return of the forward scouts. Crouched behind the thick foliage that lined the banks we watched in fascination, unable to reveal our presence and powerless to help as the drama unfolded.

A fifteen-foot crocodile lay partially hidden, basking in the late afternoon sun, its mouth agape as it sucked in rushes of air to cool itself, its soulless eyes constantly rotating as it scanned the falling water for possible prey.

A Burmese native – where he had come from or where he was going was a mystery never to be solved – oblivious of any danger, intent only in crossing the river but unable to walk because of the bottom mud, threw himself forward and began to swim with the flailing strokes of the self-taught.

Nearly a hundred yards away the basking crocodile either saw or sensed a change in the river's rhythm, and was immediately galvanized into action, pouring itself down the contours of the riverbank and entering the water without seeming to disturb the surface. It headed downstream with only its eyes and nostrils showing above the surface.

The native continued to swim towards the opposite bank, stopping now and then to recover from his untutored exertions and to check on his position.

The tidal water was now fast ebbing and he had to fight upstream to maintain his course. His actions grew more agitated as he realised he was losing ground, and instead of accepting his limitations and floating with the ebb to a different point his panic caused him to shorten his stroke, which reduced his progress even further.

The vibrations were much stronger now and the crocodile floated even closer, recognizing prey. The sweeps of its tail increasing, it thrust its giant body forward. Some thirty feet from the swimming native, it suddenly submerged for the attack and with two or three thrusts of its tail it was upon him.

Taking him from underneath it gripped a flailing leg. Unable to bite it through the crocodile suddenly spun in the water until the limb was ripped off, causing the swimmer to pirouette involuntarily. Thinking that he had snagged his foot he put his hand down to free himself. Finding nothing there, he began to scream uncontrollably and floated downstream with the receding tide.

The crocodile moved away, swallowing the leg whole without chewing, flesh and bone gulped down the giant maw in a single spasm. The man's femoral artery blossomed, pumping the life out of him, but mercifully, by this time he was dead – either from shock or drowning. The commotion, however, had attracted companion crocodiles who flung themselves into the water, eager to participate in the feast. The water boiled with the exertions of the spinning reptiles.

Nothing now remained, not even a ripple on the water. Even the blood had dissipated. There was no trace that a human being had ever existed. The show ended as the reptiles dragged themselves out of the water and onto the bank to take station once again to target the unwary.

The speed and finality of the attack had left us watchers in a state of shock and helpless, unable to reveal our position and fire in defence of the native for fear of jeopardizing our mission.

Meanwhile, the forward party had discovered a three-strand rattan bridge suspended across the *chaung* between the tallest of two opposing mango trees.

"Looks rotten to me," said Cpl. Taylor.

"Don't worry, I'll go on the rotten rattan first and if it will take my thirteen stones it should take all of you," volunteered Douglas.

Not waiting for any arguments, he took up a standing position on the central rope, and grasping the left and right ropes at shoulder height as if crucified he gingerly swayed his way to the other side, the rope dropping alarmingly to within three feet of the stinking ooze that bottomed the *chaung*. Any slip or mistake would be our last. Swallowed without trace in the primeval slime.

Half an hour later and without mishap we were on the other side and cutting our way on a more direct bearing.

The reason for the bridge became apparent after a short march. Standing in what had been a clearing, pavillioned upon rows of steps, stood an overgrown temple. The festoons of vines that had invaded from the encroaching jungle seemed to garland the temple dome and the attendant statues as if in celebration of some religious festival.

The stone-clad building stood silent in the blistering late afternoon sun, its gold and honey-coloured aspect in stark contrast to the vivid encroaching jungle.

Its half-shuttered windows seemed to droop like sleepy eyelids, suggesting a lethargy induced by the suffocating heat.

Eternally vigilant stone chintheys, mythological beasts, part lion and part griffin, ferocious in aspect, some thirty feet in height, sitting on their haunches with their front limbs stiff, flanked the entrance of the dagoba, stark and threatening to warn off evil spirits and challenging the approach of all but the faithful.

The flaming ball of the sun abandoned the day, and night with its attendant terrors stalked abroad. The warmth of the day was beginning to retreat from the temple courtyard and the opportunity to rest for the night prompted us to sleep on the steps, the stones of which, although hard and uncomfortable, would retain the heat of the day for a few hours and would be preferable to spending the night inside the temple, with the nocturnal creatures that by now were flitting in and out of the entrance.

FOURTEEN

NO ALARM CLOCK WAS NECESSARY THE FOLLOWING morning and the sentry who had stood the last watch over the sleeping men found that the dawn chorus did his job for him, as one after the other they levered themselves up from the hard steps of the temple and massaged sore and numb limbs.

"Like sleeping in a bloody bird aviary," mumbled Blackie Smith as he knocked the heels of his shoes on the ground before putting them on again. "Look at that little bastard!" he shouted, squashing a scorpion that was starting to lift its tail threateningly.

"Why didn't you let it live?" queried Tinker Taylor. "Anything that could spend a night in your shoes deserves a second chance."

After a cold breakfast, some four hours later we cut the main track we had been looking for, although it proved to be little more than a scrub-free path. However, even though our progress became appreciably easier a trodden path meant possible unwanted company and the need for caution became our first concern. Fortunately with the jungle crowding in on both sides we were virtually invisible from searching eyes. To go blundering on, however, would be suicidal so forward scouts and a rearguard were posted and set at a distance of about four hundred yards. This was no peaceful country lane we were on; it could only be traversed by foot and only then with great difficulty.

Any stores the enemy were retreating with would have to be manhandled or carried by mule. There was fresh evidence of the latter, probably only a day or two old, so our greatest fear was of an enemy ahead pulling off the track for any reason, possibly to rest or to wait for a main body to catch up.

"We'll take the mid-morning break here," remarked the Captain. "According to my calculations we seem to be making good progress." The long file of men, needing no further bidding, threw themselves down in various attitudes of complaining relief.

"Love a fag," said Daisy Green.

"Me too but we can't risk it. It would be too easily detected by a sharp nose," replied Sgt. Tighe.

The crackling of the Sergeant's handset brought all conversation to an abrupt halt. The rearguard had given them ample warning. "Party of six Japs coming up the track, sir," said the Sergeant. "Should be with us in about ten minutes."

"Right, off the track, fade into cover on both sides and we'll take them as they go past. No gunfire and no noise."

Talking animatedly amongst themselves the Japanese soldiers appeared around the bend in the track and Marines peering through the undergrowth hardly dared to breathe. Sweat ran down our faces and we did not dare to wipe it off. The waiting seemed interminable and the flies, persistently trying to drink at every rivulet of sweat, added to our torment.

Suddenly everything seemed to explode into a blur of action. As the Jap soldiers passed, the Marines pounced, too many for a clean fight, and who fights cleanly anyway when lives are on the line? Even with getting in each other's way, the action could only have one outcome. The enemy was taken completely by surprise and outnumbered. The skirmish was over in under two minutes.

"They look like schoolchildren," panted Tinker Taylor, referring to their stature.

"Don't be fooled by their size," said Capt. Newsome. "These are amongst the best jungle fighters in the world, and remember, these schoolkids, as you call them, drove the British out of Burma a couple of years ago, and would probably have taken India but for their extended supply lines. Remember also that a lot of Indians, disenchanted possibly with the British rule, would have flocked to join them, forgetting that they would be exchanging a distant governor for a tyrant. Meet them on equal terms and they will give a good account of themselves."

We picked up the dead bodies, carried them into the dense scrub, and covered them with loose brush to remove all traces from the track. Fortunately, having searched them we found no traces of means of communication, so their absence would probably not be noticed; at least, not until they were supposed to report in.

Relieving the rearguard scouts we pressed on for the remainder of the day and then camped up for the night. The comfort of the sun-warmed steps that we had enjoyed on the previous night was not for us. We sheltered beneath what rough cover we could find with a constantly dripping canopy, a pre-monsoon reminder that looked set to continue until dawn.

Sleep was impossible, and it was with some relief that the rising sun encouraged us to breakfast. As our clothes began to dry on our backs we loaded our packs once again and started to move off.

Dropping back to talk to Sgt. Tighe, Capt. Newsome calculated, "Tomorrow we should be in striking distance of our objective. If the going gets no worse I reckon we are doing better than twenty miles a day, and the men seem to be in reasonably good shape."

"Nothing but the usual bites and scratches, perhaps a touch of sunburn and sore feet, but it gives them something to moan about and keeps their minds concentrated on more trivial things. Anyway, we all know that service personnel are always 'dripping'. Wouldn't know what to do with themselves if things went perfectly," replied Tighe.

"Speaking of our targets, as we have two of them, I intend to split the force into two parts. I shall take the first group and deal with the more northerly one, which is the main production pumps, the nodding jennies, and you will take the second party and destroy the storage facilities and dumps.

"I shall be using two-hour delay fuses, to allow us to put as much distance between ourselves and the enemy as possible before the balloon goes up, but not if the success of the operation depends on more immediate action.

"You can take Taylor, Rogers, Green, Jones, Lambert, Winters, Whitehouse, Douglas and Cox, and I'll take the other nine. I'm expecting to have to deal with more dispersed targets, so any spare explosives I shall be pleased to relieve you of. Clear, Sergeant?"

"Perfectly, sir."

The sun was now directly overhead and our clothes had thoroughly dried on us. The webbing straps of our packs had begun to shrink and were rubbing and chafing. The only relief we could obtain was to sit down and lean back on them. "Like hitting your head against a brick wall," moaned Rogers. "It's heaven when you stop."

These cold comfort stops did nothing to boost morale, and the food, unimaginative and monotonous, did little more than partially fill an empty stomach, so it was with some relief and no little encouragement that we moved off again.

Some two hours later, approaching the summit of the mountain range, the ground to the left of the track suddenly appeared to have been cleared as if by a giant scythe. The scrub had been flattened and the lesser trees had been snapped off at the base of the trunks for a run of some one hundred and fifty feet.

At the end of this swathe, reared upon its engines, tail pointing to the sky and partially burnt out, stood the remains of a Dakota. The pilot, probably flying in darkness, had failed to clear the summit by a mere fifty feet.

Approaching it cautiously along the ruts that had been gouged out by its forced landing, we became aware of a sound like the swarm of angry bees. The stench was overpowering. The sight that met our eyes was beyond belief, and it took some time before our numb minds could accept the hideous panorama that unfolded before us. Even then it was too horrific to contemplate. Man's ultimate inhumanity. The sound that filled the air was from a vast cloud of flies that was swarming over some macabre meal.

"Take a look at what the little yellow bastards have done. And you called them schoolkids," said Tighe.

The Dakota pilot and his navigator had been suspended upside down by their ankles between two trees. The practice of *Bushido* – ceremonial beheading – had been performed, and the two heads had been impaled upon two stakes. The suspended torsos had been virtually cut from the crotch to the neck by a ceremonial sword, forming a hideous 'V' sign. Rigor mortis had obviously come and gone. The heads and lower torsos were blue-green and streaked with black where the blood had accumulated and congealed.

Large clusters of insect eggs hung from their eyes, open mouths and nostrils like bunches of developing grapes. Fully developed maggots had eaten most of the more accessible flesh and entrails that had spilled from the violated bodies that now hung as if in some obscene abattoir. The ground beneath them was crawling with bloated maggots vainly searching for the meal that they had recently fallen from.

We had seen death in many forms during our service and had quickly acquired immunity at the sight of it. You had to or you couldn't carry on, but it was not the close-up view or the horror of the advanced decomposition that affected us, but the all-pervading stench that drenched the senses and from which there was no escape.

The need for haste was still paramount, particularly as the perpetrators could only be two or three days ahead on the trail, but we couldn't leave before we removed the grotesque and hideous 'V' signs. Throwing caution to the wind, we collected enough dried grass and small branches to build a fire beneath each corpse, and the flames and smoke combined were sufficient to disperse the plague of flies long enough for the bodies to be cut down, wrapped in groundsheets, and roughly buried.

The only identification possible was on the plane's fuselage, which fortunately remained intact.

The feeling of revulsion and anger that settled on us as we continued on the march persisted for some few miles, and the very silence boded ill for the perpetrators of so vile an act. Our expressions mirrored the full realization of the type of enemy we were up against – merciless, ruthless and totally without humanity. What kind of society could spawn a practice of such bestial cruelty?

The acts of barbarism that hadn't been seen in the western world since the end of the Dark Ages were totally abhorrent and alien to civilised behaviour. *Bushido* might have been acceptable to Japanese culture, but together with the ill-treatment of prisoners and of subjugated peoples that had its more recent roots in the invasion and rape of China, it was seemingly being perpetrated by choice, not necessity.

Late in the evening saw us looking down on a small valley. Either side of the tracks were marked with thin plumes of smoke that collected and hung like blue caps over the tall canopy.

"Rest here and we'll investigate under cover of darkness," said the Captain. "Could be a village."

"I'd love a cup of char and a hot meal," said Taffy Jones.

"More likely to be another class of your schoolkids," replied his mate. "I hope it's the bastards we're looking for. What I wouldn't give to destroy that schoolkids' simile once and for all."

Darkness was accompanied by the usual chorus of bullfrogs.

"Like a bloody night shift coming on," commented Jack Douglas. After the birdsong and calls of the day you could practically set your watch by the change. No twilight, no afterglow; just daylight or darkness.

Now that the darkness had cloaked the day, the night mists rose from the ground to provide an eerie stage, treacherous for walking but ideal for our purpose, so Tinker Taylor and Bob Rogers were detailed to push forward down the trail towards the source of the smoke to investigate.

"Looks like some rest or transit camp area," whispered Rogers as they crouched together in the damp scrub. "Everyone seems relaxed; no sentries out. They must feel pretty secure and sure of themselves. I make it two rows of four-man tents either side of the track. Totalling twenty-six in all, and if they are all full we're talking of upwards of more than one hundred men. Think we've seen enough. Let's get back and give them something to worry about."

The Captain digested the scouts' report. "Too far to go around, and too noisy to cut a loop track. We shall have to go through," he said. "We need to be five miles further down the road by midnight so that we can lie up for the final push." He seemed to gloss over the problems and make it appear so matter-of-fact that the confidence seemed to rub off on all of us.

"I make that five each," said Daisy Green to no one in particular, and getting no response, he assumed that we were all mulling over the same privilege in private.

Later, following Taylor and Rogers down to the valley floor, we approached the split camp and selected the group of tents furthest away from the track for our first attention. Working in pairs we lifted the tent flap, and as if by numbers, as in training, one placed a big hand across the sleeping man's mouth whilst his partner slid a knife, firmly and gently into his chest. No sound; death came like a thief in the night, uninvited and totally unexpected.

Thirteen tents and twenty minutes later there were fifty-two men dead, some small satisfaction for the outrage against the Dakota's crew. The only diversion had come when a rib deflected a knife thrust and Bob Rogers had to lie across the victim's flailing legs whilst his mate struck again and again with the knife in an effort to silence him.

It was all very well looking down a rifle barrel and seeing an enemy fall, but a totally different matter to feel his hot breath upon you and to dispatch him by hand. It became a personal thing and seemed to diminish both the act and the reason, however necessary.

Close combat was a different thing again. The fact that the enemy had the same chance as you seemed acceptable, although practice, skill and surprise would give you the edge. The superiority instilled in distant basic training lent that quiet confidence that was a necessary ingredient for success.

"Things are going too well," said the Captain. "Let's move over the trail and do some more house calls while the bastards are asleep. It only needs for some insomniac to go for a midnight stroll."

"They aren't all asleep," whispered Douglas. "Someone's sitting on the bog."

Making a motion of a throat being cut, Tighe detailed him to attend to the threat, and whilst the remainder of men sank out of sight in the scrub to wait in silence Douglas slipped quietly into the shadows. Gripping his knife between his teeth he approached the makeshift latrine, which was no more than a log thrown over a deep hole.

Creeping up behind the unsuspecting Jap he threw his arm around his throat to cut off any sound and slid the knife in behind his ear and into his brain. Withdrawing the knife, he allowed the body to slide slowly backwards, before he got covered in blood, into the deep pit where it disappeared beneath the surface.

Douglas crawled back to the waiting men, having cleaned his knife by pushing it into the ground. His mate whispered, "Hope you let him finish," but Douglas's reply was lost as the file of men moved over the track to the next row of tents.

Moving like clockwork the deadly work continued until someone tripped over a guy rope and knocked a cooking pot flying. Then all hell broke loose. A burst of automatic fire cut down two of the Marines, then Tighe, taking the situation in at a glance, ran towards the confusion. Seeing a Jap outlined against the inside of the tent, he knifed him through the canvas.

The pale light of dawn saw us taking stock, and it was decided to leave the camp shipshape and intact to give the impression that the enemy were in transit. The dead soldiers were carried deep into the forest and obscured from view. All the equipment and ammunition, together with rifles and grenades, were wrapped in waterproof groundsheets and buried. These could be needed on the way back. A detail had cleaned up the kitchen area and left the pots and pans in order. The bloodstained canvas and tear site where Douglas had knifed the enemy was scorched to destroy any evidence.

Everyone expressed themselves satisfied with what they saw. The Captain said under his breath, "I hope they swallow this story we're leaving them, or they'll be all over our tails like angry hornets."

The two British casualties were wrapped up in blankets and buried, minus dog-tags, and the site of their graves, although obscured, was recorded. Standing bare-headed for a few moments, the Captain seemed to mumble something about, "The transience of this mortal life, flowers in a field being cut down", but each man was deep in his own thoughts and responded only to the "Amen".

With scarcely a backward glance at comrades left behind beneath the towering cathedral-like canopy of trees, we picked up our equipment and moved out of the camp area, but the thought that we had left something of ourselves behind was uppermost in our own minds.

"Three down, seventeen to go," muttered Bob Rogers to Stan Whitehouse, who had fallen in beside him.

"Well, how long do you want to live?" Stan countered. "Think of what you've got to go home to. The Germans are bombing the hell out of Britain, the Yanks are screwing your missus, and your job's been given to a conchie."

"Sorry I spoke. So I'm better off out here; I didn't realize I was so lucky."

"Save your breath for something useful," said Tighe, coming up behind them. "Take the forward point."

"Thanks, Sarge, then I can die alone."

"Don't mention it, but report in before you do." Anything else Tighe might have said was lost in the sound of his *panga* as he cut his way back onto the track.

FIFTEEN

STAN WHITEHOUSE COULDN'T REMEMBER A TIME WHEN he had not wanted to join the services. At senior school after lessons, he would make his way to the local railway station and watch with wonder at the service personnel returning from leave with their kit bags over their shoulders. These were the regulars; conscription hadn't been enforced yet, and the war had yet to be declared, but everyone knew it was coming.

This was 1936 and Germany was rearming, and had been for years – Britain was pretending it wasn't happening and turned a blind eye. Churchill was warning the Government but it was all falling on deaf ears, and the phoney war was with us.

When he had left school at fourteen, he had naturally gravitated to the 'Pot Bank', the foremost local employer, Royal Doulton Potteries, Nile Street, Burslem. His particular duty was to operate the 'sand shaker', a dusty, noisy machine that extracted the metal particles from the sand that were used by the 'placers' to pack cups, saucers and porcelain figurines in the 'saggers' (fireclay boxes) prior to firing in the kilns. This occupation was unskilled, heavy and dangerous, and brought with it a free pint of milk per day to guard against consumption. When the kilns were unloaded and the wares taken out, the sand was emptied, collected and delivered to the shakers and the process started all over again.

The monotony, and a doctor's advice to get out of the dusty environment because of a persistent cough, encouraged him to look further afield (direction of labour had not yet come into force). He found employment with a bakery in Tunstall.

Shortages due to rationing were forgotten in his new employment. It was like putting a child into a sweet shop. Bread and cakes, all in short supply and rationed by shortages, except rejects, misshapes and failures, were avidly collected and taken home to supplement the meagre rations.

After a while the working hours began to pall. It was a 6 a.m. start and 6 p.m. finish six days a week, Monday to Saturday; a total of seventy-two hours for the princely sum of 12^s/6^d.

Living in the country, there was no transport at that time in the morning, so a walk across the fields from Norton to Tunstall added a further hour each way. A total of eighty-six hours, and with ten shillings given to his mother for his keep, the 2^s/6^d he had left over was just enough to buy him a packet of fags and a couple of pints of beer.

The problem was resolved for Whitehouse when at seventeen-and-a-half years of age he had to register for National Service. Then, a few weeks later, he was called for his medical, and being graded A1 he could express a preference for the service he fancied, although they tried to talk him into going down the mines.

The only way they would get him to go underground was when he was dead, although someone had to do it, and later people would be conscripted and couldn't refuse. 'Bevin Boys', as they became known, were there to support the war effort, more and more coal being required. This labour shortage would also be met by the Polish communities that were escaping Nazi occupation of their country.

His final choice was the Royal Marines, and all he had to do now was to wait for his call-up papers and discover where he had to report to. 18^s/6^d per week and all found was preferable to his present job and he couldn't wait. He looked forward to the uniform and the unlimited travel and adventure.

Time being short, he made the most of his home life with his parents and two younger brothers, the latter quite envious of the adventure he was looking forward to. His girlfriend of a few months promised to write to him, but he didn't hold out much hope. The Yanks had a lot to offer – silk stockings, chocolate and a seemingly endless supply of money. Cynical perhaps, but realistic.

When visiting the local Palais the floor was crowded as usual and they remarked that there were no longer the rows of 'Wallflowers' – girls waiting to be asked to dance – seated around the edge of the room. This problem no longer existed. Gum-chewing Yanks demonstrated their dexterity and prowess, jiving and jitterbugging, their partners wide-eyed and breathless, having a marvellous time and fully captivated.

British servicemen unable to find partners were heard to remark, "The girls think they are all bloody film stars. When they go away, we shall be left to pick up the pieces, and the little bastards! I think they suffer from the 'overs'. They're overpaid, oversexed, overactive, overbearing and over here."

"Letting off steam, I suppose, but so brash and in your bloody face. I suppose they've come over here to win the war for us, two years too late, but Uncle Sam doesn't do anything for nothing. Our children will still be paying these debts off in fifty years' time."

"There will only be one winner in this war monetarily and that's America. She will come out of it richer than when she went in due to her overwhelming industrial might. Lend lease? We're leasing our souls! Churchill will put our family silver into hock for the next couple of generations."

"To their credit, however, they are cheerfully putting their lives on the line, believing like we do that it's the next man who gets it, never you."

The midday meal was eaten on the march to make up for the time lost at the site of the plane crash and in the Jap camp. It was taken from 'K' rations – dried biscuits, a small jar of fish paste, two squares of chocolate, water purifying tablets, two cigarettes, four matches and four pieces of toilet paper.

"I bet the prat who thought up this repast is dining at the Ritz on lobster, a dozen oysters and all the trimmings, strawberries, and a bottle of Chablis, seated opposite an impressionable blonde," moaned Taffy Jones.

"Probably your missus," remarked someone, who had to duck as an empty jar of fish paste whistled past his ear.

"Don't leave that lying around. We don't want to broadcast our presence," said Tighe.

The last meal of rice and fish (courtesy of the Japanese cooks), to which we had helped ourselves before we left the camp, was beginning to have dire consequences, and our progress was severely curtailed as first one and then another left the trail for the privacy of the forest.

"Better stay here overnight. We can't carry on like this. Get off the track and bivvy down."

Setting two-hour watches we snatched what rest we could. We awoke to find the Captain and Sergeant deep in conversation.

"Another good day's march should see us down into the foothills, and it's at this point we'll split up. Take your party to within a safe distance from the refinery and plan your move from there. If we both go in at midnight with two-hour fuses we should be back out again before anyone realizes we've been, and far enough away to be reasonably safe. We can rendezvous back at this point tomorrow night, wait for a day for either party to rejoin, but move out independently if necessary and make our own way back. As we have discussed before I think our best way back is to head for Cox's Bazaar, as I expect the track to be rather busy by then. However, play it by ear, and if we are unable for whatever reason to wait for each other, do what you have to do to get out. The important objective, in fact the only objective, is to destroy those fuel dumps."

SIXTEEN

AFTER THE ENFORCED OVERNIGHT STOP DUE TO the after-effects of our last meal of fish and rice, courtesy of the late Japanese cooks, we sanitized the area and prepared to set off again.

The short straws had been drawn by Bob Donnelly and Bob Ketley, both Devon men from the South Hams, and they were posted as forward scouts. Their accents, strange to their companions, and often the butt of "ooh ahh" jokes, earned them their nicknames of 'Scrumpy' and 'Cider' for obvious reasons.

They made their way on both sides of the track a couple of hundred yards ahead of the main body. Feeling very comfortable with each other, originating from the same neck of the woods back home, their conversation tended to be about their local Hams, Chillington and Slapton.

"Got a letter from Mom before we left Chittagong," said Scrumpy. "It appears that practically all the area has been evacuated. They've all been sent to accommodations further inland. Something to do with the present emergency, I suppose. Couldn't say much, didn't know much, but it's something to do with the Yanks."

"Heard much the same myself. Wonder what the hell's going on?"

Lost deep in their own thoughts they continued to push on at a remorseless pace with the full intention of achieving their full twenty miles.

What they didn't know was that the whole of the South Hams from Torcross to Street had been completely evacuated of civilians and livestock, all in the space of six weeks.

More than 700 families and some 180 farms had been cleared in those six weeks so that the American troops could move in to set up camp and strong-points, completely isolating them from the rest of the population.

Homes were stripped by the outgoing families; all usable crops were dug up and removed to storage further inland. The locals were given help with the heaviest of furniture, farm equipment and livestock, the latter being moved to farms further inland beyond the commandeered area. These farmers were glad both to share their fields and to house the livestock of the incomers during the emergency.

All the Devonians joined in to help the displaced civilians and to relocate them and their families. The hospitals opened their doors to the sick and elderly, and the children, many of whom had already been evacuated to the South Hams because of the air raids in London and Plymouth, found themselves being uprooted again and resettled with strangers.

Churches were stripped of their priceless plate and religious artefacts. The fine wood traceries were packed into wooden crates and stored for the duration. Stained-glass windows were sandbagged up together with items that couldn't be moved, such as fonts, pulpits and doors. When the churches had been secured and vacated, the following notice, signed by Charles, Bishop of Exeter, was displayed:

> TO OUR ALLIES OF THE U.S.A. This church has stood here for several hundred years. Around it has grown a community, which has lived in these houses and tilled these fields ever since there was a church. This church, this churchyard, in which their loved ones lie at rest, these homes, these fields, are as dear to those who have left them as are the homes and graves and fields which you, our Allies, have left behind you. They hope to return one day, as you hope to return to yours, to find them waiting to welcome them home. They entrust them to your care meanwhile and pray that God's blessing may rest upon us all.
> Charles, Bishop of Exeter

The six weeks soon passed and the villages became ghost-like. Streets and lanes where villagers had previously congregated and chatted were silent; weeds began to take over the gardens, and the fields where cattle had grazed were empty.

The American forces began billeting in the vacant hotels, schools and properties. Armed guards began to patrol the streets and country lanes; they were also patrolling the whole of the perimeter to prevent entry from the civilian population.

The whole area had been chosen because of the similarities to the proposed invasion beaches of France.

Nissen huts and tents sprang up all around the area to house the burgeoning number of troops. Quays, jetties and yards were built to service the hundreds of ships and landing craft.

During a major exercise between US and British landing craft, five craft from Plymouth and three from Brixham were attacked by German E-boats of the 5th and 9th Schnellboote Flotillas based at Cherbourg. The result was carnage. Some 700 sailors and soldiers were killed, mainly drowned, a lot of them inexperienced youngsters who were wearing their lifejackets back to front, which forced their heads under water. Compounding it all, the US and British ships couldn't talk to each other as their radio frequencies didn't mesh.

An immediate news blackout was enforced around the whole area and no discussions were allowed outside the exclusion zone, which would prove difficult to enforce as bodies were being washed ashore for days. Also, there was no need to give the enemy's morale a boast, and the facts would probably not be disclosed until after the war.

Who was supposed to provide the naval screen for this exercise?

Who was supposed to coordinate the radios?

All this was happening on the other side of the world and Scrumpy and Cider knew nothing of it.

Meanwhile the file of men followed each other, intent only on putting one foot in front of the other. The only break in the monotony was when they were forced to cross the swollen rivers, up to their armpits, and to help each other over the slippery outcrops of stones.

Night fell and they made a night stop to rest up for the final push to the target the next day.

The only cause for concern was that Jess Lambert had gone missing. A couple of the lads had gone back to search for him, but with no luck. They had to give it up after a couple of hours. Probably the mystery would never be solved.

Seventeen

D ENNY GREEN AND I HAD TAKEN UP the rearguard some two hundred
yards behind the long file of men that stretched into the distance.
The undulating nature of the terrain, together with the natural barri-
ers created by the rock and scree outcrops and the encroaching jungle, caused
the column to disappear and reappear as if riding a rollercoaster.

Signalling to my mate that I was about to disappear into the undergrowth
for a little privacy, I left the track and picked my way between the towering
trees until I had sufficient distance for my purpose.

Snapping open my webbing belt and undoing my shoulder epaulettes, I
shrugged off my heavy pack and allowed it to slide to the floor.

Startled suddenly by the commotion of fluttering wings above me I stumbled backwards, tripped over my pack, and cracked my head against the trunk
of a tree. My legs buckled beneath me and I fell and rolled into the only patch
of sun for many yards. When I came round, I was lying in shade, the sun having
completed its arc.

What time had elapsed, my confused mind refused to grasp, but the sun had
taken its toll. I had the delicate skin of all redheads, and even short exposure
to the sun had severe consequences. My lips had erupted in blisters and one
side of my face felt as if it was burning. The sweat that had accumulated on my
forehead ran down my cheeks, finding the cracked skin, but due to the soreness,
I was unable to wipe it off. My exploring fingers traced the blisters on my
eyelids, down the sides of my face and along both lips.

Dry throat and swollen tongue screamed out for water, but there was no use
in checking my bottle. That had been empty for the last two days.

I picked up my pack and tommy gun and slung them over my shoulder,
wincing at the weight and pain. I set off in the direction of the saddle pass, to
try to catch up with the column.

After about half a mile of upward slope the track suddenly widened as a small plateau of tableland came into view. I continued to walk in the shadow of the trees as long as I was able to, and then broke out into the open ground.

The sun hit the side of my face with a sledgehammer blow but the heat lacked the venom it had possessed at noon. Still, I slanted my bush hat to create what shade it afforded and felt marginally better for it.

I was about one hundred yards onto the plateau when the Japanese soldiers came into view. I had heard them from behind first, from a distance, as they talked and laughed amongst themselves.

The Japanese soldiers and I saw each other at the same moment, and with full-throated shouts, they lifted their rifles and loosed off three shots in my direction.

I didn't hear the bullets thud into anything as I broke into a lung-bursting run. I mentally shook off the impulse to look back at my pursuers, my mind working quite logically in spite of the fear of death that invaded my conscious-ness. Forty, thirty, twenty, the yards flew by beneath my racing feet; long yards to the cover of the rocks. Fourth and fifth shots rang out and chips and shards of rock spat back at me as I dived headlong for protection to the side of a boulder, and then scrambled around to the back of it.

I had thrown my pack and tommy gun ahead of me as I dived for cover, and they had fallen out of reach some thirty feet below. Knowing the exact position of the enemy would be of little use as I could only fight effectively at close quarters. Cursing my luck at being unable to retrieve the pack and tommy gun without exposing my position, I brought my right knee up and found the knife tucked into the top of my boot. Then flat on my stomach, I crawled to the side, from the cover of one protective boulder to another.

Beyond the loose scree was a deep sand ridge and I went over and down to the other side. The depressions my feet and hands made created telltale signs of my passing. Sand trickled into them, but not sufficient to fill them.

The soldiers had stopped, uncertain of where I was or how I was armed, and I had a vivid picture of them as I continued on all fours, scampering crabwise along the sand depression towards the more secure cover of the rearing rocks and defiles.

There was a burst of excited talk, then the staccato sound of an authoritative voice, then silence. There would be no rushing forward. They considered that they had their quarry cornered and would therefore proceed with all caution and stealth as they closed in for the kill.

The sand ridge that had afforded me cover suddenly ended at the rock face. The rise of ground to my right had no appreciable cover, so I had to move suddenly and fast. For a good fifteen yards, I would be in full view. However, I would be a moving target and I would be doing something positive, my way. If I remained inactive and waiting, I could only respond. Not a good idea; the first soldier over the sand ridge would have me like a pig in an entry.

The overriding desire to survive nullified the feeling of total exhaustion brought on by my overexposure to the sun. I rolled over onto one knee, my other leg thrust out behind me. I gulped in a lungful of air and exploded into a low run like a sprinter starting from the blocks.

I had covered about one third of the distance to my goal when the first soldier to spot me shouted and loosed off a shot that ploughed into sand alongside my running feet, but now with more solid ground beneath my feet, I began to move faster, dodging from left to right to present a more difficult target. The sun in which I had lain exposed for almost four hours hadn't completely drained the moisture from my body. Suddenly there was an excess, a reserve stored up for fear, and now I was using it up. It oozed from me in unrestrained rivulets.

I had reached cover now, and quite soon, the Sons of Heaven would be upon me, which was my aim. I could only retaliate at close quarters. Cursing again my luck at losing my tommy gun, I drew my knife from the leg of my boot and placed it between my teeth, leaving my hands free for climbing; my mouth was forced into a leering grin where my teeth gripped the blade.

I reached high above my head and began to climb, pulling myself, hand over hand, up the pitted rock face at right angles to the approaching danger. My breath began to whistle and gasp over the flat blade of the knife, and unaffordable saliva ran down my chin, blending with fluid that drained from the burst sun blisters on my eyelids and cheeks.

"Come on, you slanty-eyed little bastards, do your worst," I hissed over the flat blade of my knife.

Suddenly, one of the soldiers who had decided to outflank me found an adjacent place to climb and appeared slowly over the rock summit. First, his reaching, gripping hands, then the back of his head and shoulders came into view, straining as he attempted to pull himself over the top.

Taking the knife from my mouth I wiped the blade down my leg, my arm bent backwards, then suddenly flexed forward, the thumb and forefinger opened, and the long heavy knife spun blade over handle across the intervening thirty feet.

It was the much-practised throw of my weapon of choice, and it found its mark left of centre and buried itself to the hilt in the climbing man's back. The soldier screamed and doubled forward against the invasion of steel, scrabbling frantically with his hands but unable to drag his weight over the rim. He fell back to the scree below and was dead before the shale he disturbed had finished moving.

Now I had lost my knife. What followed had to be pure improvisation. I lowered myself to the bottom of the rock face, knowing the exact position of the enemy wouldn't help me. With no offensive weapon I had to wait for them to come to me, so I mentally shook off the impulse to look around for them.

Pressing myself into a recess in the rock face, I loosened my leather waist belt, the only other form of weapon I possessed. Holding it in my left hand I allowed it to hang down, weighted by the heavy brass buckle. I must have waited a full fifteen minutes, which seemed like an eternity, but I considered the pause was to my advantage. My muscles, stiffened by the inactivity, worried me and any flexing that I could do was limited and could only be peripheral for fear of betraying my position.

Suddenly my ears detected movement; the sound of measured footsteps, cautious but oncoming. I stiffened preparatory to explosive action; the footsteps were too close together to suggest a single enemy. How many? Two, three? One I could cope with; two would be difficult. Any more and I would need some kind of divine intervention.

My sideway's glance took in two soldiers as they shuffled cautiously towards me, crouching forward. The leading one was armed with the plain sword of an NCO, which he held out before him. His comrade some fifteen feet behind him brandished a rifle with a fixed bayonet that he carried at the high port. All these details registered in my mind subconsciously as I tensed myself to take the initiative.

The leading soldier was the first to see me, and as he opened his mouth to shout a warning, it was at this precise moment I was galvanized into action. Realizing that my adversary had to raise his sword arm to slash or draw it back to thrust, I whirled my belt around my opponent's neck, caught the buckle as it came back to me, and drew the startled man towards me, holding him in a bear-like hug beneath the arms.

His companion close behind stopped and fired instinctively from the hip, a purely reflex action, as I whirled the NCO towards him using him as a shield. The bullet struck him in the back.

As he started to slump to the floor I pushed the now limp body away from me towards the advancing Japanese, who had dropped his rifle and drawn his sword for close combat, raising it to slash downwards. At the same moment, the dead body smashed into him. He yelled and staggered backwards into the rock face.

I launched myself forward after the dead body had crashed to the ground, scooping up the fallen man's knife as I went forward. The soldier, although badly winded, raised his sword above his head with a yell half of terror and half of anger. Bending low, I came in under the sword stroke, taking it on the flat of my back, where its force and lethal effect was dissipated.

Gripping him in a bear-like hug beneath the armpits, my forward momentum smashed the lighter Japanese against the rock face, knocking the wind out of him. The knife that I had taken from his dead companion was now positioned point first against my opponent's back. Drawing him back, I repeated the lunge against the side of the rock and the blade was driven deep between his shoulder blades.

Shock and surprise were complete. His lips curled to reveal black and rotten teeth and his foul breath fanned across my face. Blood welled up and foamed between his lips as the knife found a lung, and he began to choke on his own gore.

Breaking away from my opponent as his knees began to buckle I allowed him to slide to the ground, the knife still lodged in his back, scraping against the rock, before he finally fell flat on his back, driving the blade to protrude grotesquely through his chest. There was no plea or expectation of mercy and the eyes that stared back at his executioner were two dark pools of pain, centred by hatred.

As I picked up the fallen man's sword, my every movement was followed by my quarry's eyes. They lifted up, following my upraised arm as it went sideways to shoulder height, and accepted the inevitable as it was brought down in a slashing movement across the prostrate man's throat.

Flies clustered to feed on the fresh blood, and some landed on my chest to drink from the crimson stains that had splashed onto my tunic. They arose quickly and buzzed angrily away as I brushed my hand across myself.

Sinking down on my knees in complete exhaustion, my hands still gripping the sword hilt, I forced the stained blade slowly into the sand as I allowed my head to rest on my crossed wrists.

I was fighting for breath and too weak to stand up, but at the back of my mind calmer forces were accumulating my thoughts, suggesting that this was not a good place in which to linger.

How long I remained in the position of rest whilst I indulged the multitude of pains in my limbs and body I would never know, but I was brought suddenly to earth by the pain from my lips, which had cracked open during my recent exertions, and the raging thirst that seared my throat with every breath.

Opening my eyes, I surveyed the recent carnage, my gaze flicking over each corpse, subconsciously searching for anything that would contribute to my own wellbeing. Three water bottles were the only extra weight I considered carrying, and shaking them each in turn, I was delighted to find them nearly full.

Uncorking the first one, I lifted it to my lips and started to drink. The first swallow took me completely by surprise. The liquid burned my throat. I gagged once, then again, and shouted in pain as the liquid trickled out of my mouth and over my cracked lips.

The little bastards had filled their bottles with sake!

Criminal, I cursed, *should have been bloody shot*, and then I smiled grimly to myself at the irony of my thoughts.

However, it was some kind of fluid and if used judicially and sparingly it would serve me well enough although the permutations made the mind boggle. I thought wryly of crackers and fish paste with sake, corned beef and sake, although I would willingly have swapped all three bottles of alcohol for one of sweet water.

I had to get rid of all evidence of the recent action. I dragged the three corpses by the feet and rolled them down over the sand ridge, throwing their equipment in after them. The only thing that I retained was the sword and scabbard, even though to be caught by the Japanese with one in your possession meant instant death. The sand and shale were hot to my touch but it took little effort to push them over them, obliterating all traces of their presence.

Without a backward glance I retrieved and cleaned my knife by thrusting it into the sand, picked up my pack and tommy gun from where they had landed, and strode off purposefully, mentally acknowledging that I was at least four hours behind the main column and would have to continue far into the night to catch up.

The only thing in my favour was that the sun, my tormentor, was beginning to set and the oven-like blasts of air would give way to an equally unpleasant night. Darkness would bring with it an intense cold, which in its own way would be as cruel as the heat of the day.

When I had been picked for this mission no one had promised an easy ride. Quite the contrary; it was probably a one-way ticket, and that would have to be paid for personally. Still, it was how one travelled, not the length of the journey, that was important, and looking back over my shoulder I smiled to myself, and the blisters that framed my mouth erupted into new spasms of pain as they split into cracks, reminding me that at least for the moment I was travelling on. Shading my questing eyes I squinted into the far distance, trying to unlock its capacity for deceit, not knowing what was around the corner.

EIGHTEEN

NIGHT FELL SUDDENLY IN THE HIGH MOUNTAINS. There was no twilight and the still air quickly took on the keen edge of pre-frost. The sky remained cloudless, inviting the cold, and the canopy of night was bright with the clustered pinpoints of myriad stars.

The gibbous moon elevated herself, and because the heat haze had dissipated I could see into the far distance more clearly than during the day. My progress was quite rapid, but without breaking into a trot.

I knew that I must drive myself forward although my strength should have failed me long before. There comes a time when you call upon reserves that are vastly overdrawn and the only thing that keeps you going is habit and sheer bloody-mindedness.

I was now climbing steadily upwards and the muscles in my legs began to tighten with the effort. Mind over matter, I decided, was the thing; think about something else other than the pain and cramps that were attaching themselves to my limbs. I lowered my subconscious into a walking mechanical trance, one foot in front of the other.

The sixteen hours that had elapsed since we had broken morning camp seemed light years away. Such was my state of mind and concentration, I forgot who I was, forgot what I was doing here. I even forgot where I was going. Minutes stretched into quarter-hours, then into hours. I was totally unaware of the passage of time, then finally oblivious of my surroundings.

Suddenly I felt myself being supported on either side and hearing a voice from a long way off saying, "You're going the right way to get yourself bloody shot. Where the hell have you been? Did you have to go all the way back to base camp to find a loo?"

It meant nothing to me, and I didn't hear them explain that two of them had backtracked and looked for me for a couple of hours before finally giving up the search, unable to explain my disappearance.

I pitched forward, finally relieved of the need to think for myself, and was asleep before I hit the ground. It was still dark when I came round and it was the intense cold that finally shook the cobwebs away. All was silent except for the chattering of my teeth. I shut my mouth tightly and concentrated on controlling my shaking limbs. This took some time and the next step was to recall how I got here.

Three bottles of sake took some explaining, together with the sword, and there were some raised eyebrows when I said that "I had been invited to a Japanese party."

Gradually the voices seemed to get further away, the immediate images blurred with the dark background, and I was asleep again.

The morning watch sentry shook me by the shoulders and I snapped my eyes open and squinted against the invasion of the sun. Although the period of sleep had been relatively short, I had slept naturally and had awakened with total recall. My whole body felt rested and in spite of the pain that was registering from every part of myself I stood up, stretched myself, flexed my shoulders, tested my leg muscles and pronounced myself fit. Whatever I did, for however long, was all a bonus. In fact, every day was a bonus.

The sun was hot, just as hot as it had been yesterday, and the day before. The only difference was the date, but now we were psychologically attuned to handle it, and better still, we had a little liquid, even though it was only sake.

We moved in single file, eyes probing steadily up towards the jagged mountain peaks that reared up in a succession of naturally distorted sculptures, attainable but menacing in aspect viewed through the heat haze that shimmered in the far distance. The mirages flashed and glistened first left then right, but they were only optical illusions generated by the intense heat that had any movement at all.

A meal break at midday seemed an unwelcome interlude, with only dry biscuits and bully beef, until someone produced a can of peaches that was shared out, each man spearing a segment with his jackknife. The syrup, too cloying and sweet on its own, was diluted with one of the bottles of sake, each man taking a swallow in turn from the jagged rim of the can. It burned its way down the throat, but after being deprived of water for so long it was welcomed, like nectar of the gods.

To this point, the route had been steadily upwards over broken ground and intercepting gullies, but now we were approaching rolling foothills where our progress would become progressively more tortuous.

At the top of the first rise, we could look down on the greenery of the dense canopy that shrouded the valley floor, and the whole appearance was one of a benign, verdant Eden, deceptive in its primeval beauty and deadly in its destructive capacity.

There had been no need to hurry to this point. Another day should have been enough to see us well within the time scale. It was now midway through the afternoon and the sun was still projecting its violence from the cloudless dome of the sky. The need to find some shade on the way down to the valley floor became paramount. The prospect of finding some water down below lent some immediate purpose to our march.

Sweet water was always a problem as there was a limit to what each man could carry. Tapping and splitting the tall bamboo that abounded in generous stands, some as thick as a man's thigh, could be relied on to provide enough to quench a thirst, and the evil-smelling sumps that the buffalo wallowed in would supply sufficient for tea-making, provided the forest tinder was sufficiently dry to make a smokeless fire. The inoculations against typhoid, cholera and typhus had been given before setting out and the water sterilizing tablets saved us from dysentery.

Without the luxury of water to wash in we quickly became dirty enough to suit the most pernickety and demanding louse. The discovery of lice caused a feeling of revulsion, but very quickly we accepted their presence and took them for granted, and during meal breaks or bivouac lice-picking contests were held and a prize of sweets or cigarettes was given to the man with the highest score.

The lice seemed to doze quietly whilst we were on the march. The thought of them could be tolerated just as long as there was sufficient daylight at the end of the day's march for us to light the nub of a candle and run it up the inside seams of our shirts, delighting in the popping sounds as the flame seared and burst our tormentors.

Sometimes we arrived at a bivouac after dusk, and it took an exhausted man with a very tough skin to sleep with the lice crawling around, making a meal of him in the most inaccessible of places. Where they were designed to fit into the general scheme of things is one of life's mysteries, but the ticks seemed to team with the lice to make sleep impossible.

Tick heads remain in the skin for life and years later would have to be removed surgically, and we quickly learned not to try to pull them off by hand, as the head would break off, but to touch the body with a lighted cigarette.

The constantly dripping canopy coupled with the fording of swamps, and our clothes became wet enough to attract the repulsive leeches that attached themselves to any unprotected skin, gorging themselves on blood until, unable to drink any more, they fell down on the insides of both shirts and trousers where they exploded, spreading the donor's blood back upon them.

The forest floor was never still for a second, day or night. The vermin that scurried through it during the day merely gave way to a night shift of equal persistence and venom. Finding a bivouac free from all pests was a sheer impossibility, but so long as it was free from red and white ants and scorpions it was considered acceptable.

The red ants were up to three quarters of an inch long, very offensive, and possessed a needle-sharp bite. White ants were not so aggressive but had a penchant for clothing and equipment and would quickly leave a trail of havoc through a pack. Loose or casual stones had to be turned over to disturb the scorpions that had scuttled under them during the day.

This was no English country lane stroll; this environment could kill and the ill-prepared or unwary or careless seldom got a second chance. The remains of many a marauding careless creature were ample proof of this. A single traveller would stand no chance and would very easily become a meal for one of the many predators that lay in wait for the unwary. Such was the terrain through which we had to pass, but with our strength in numbers and firepower we felt relatively secure.

Nineteen

CAUTION ENFORCED BY THE THINNING OF COVER as we approached our objective made progress noticeably slower, and it was far into the evening when the party split up to reach their separate objectives.

"Assuming that the Japanese set the same watches as ourselves, wait for the change at midnight, which should give three clear hours to do what we have come to do," said the Captain. "Good luck. See you back under the green umbrella in about six hours' time."

"Thank you, sir, and the same to you," replied Sgt. Tighe, his cheerfulness belying his inward feelings as he watched half of his comrades fade into the approaching night.

The last few miles were slow and laborious and it wasn't until 22:00 hours that we were in full sight of our objective, viewed from the edge of the jungle that the Japanese hadn't cleared.

A fitful scudding moon revealed the details to Sgt. Tighe, lying prone, scanning the base minutely through his night sights. Four thirty-foot sentry towers, built mainly out of bamboo, were strategically placed at the corners of the compound, and a sentry walking around the top platform would have an uninterrupted view to the next one.

Five long, low buildings situated on the far side of the site, raised on stilts to lift them clear of water during the monsoon season and keep them cool during the heat of the day, were probably living accommodation. A single cabin-like structure to one side was probably the radio shack judging by the two poles nearby, which probably carried an aerial strung between them.

Set on its own and of a more substantial structure, and also patrolled by two armed guards, was the building most likely to be the explosive store.

Sweeping his sights further afield he saw what at first he took to be rows of tents, then suddenly realized he was looking at serried rows of canvas-sided vehicles, parked side by side and nose to tail on a piece of ground half the size of a football pitch. *Must be upwards of a hundred and fifty trucks there*, he mused, *probably assembled to do a Dunkirk for the retreating Japs*.

"They are parked in what appears to be a dried-up paddy field," he said, talking it over with his men. "That explains what the earthen embankments are around the perimeter."

The storage tanks stood stark and massive against a backdrop of scudding clouds, eight in all, in two rows of four, the last one backing onto the transport park.

The moon had now disappeared, leaving a cold and miserable night. The rising mists swirled to waist height, obscuring the ground and forcing extreme caution in finding a sure footing. The whole party, now embraced in these wet mists, moved like disembodied spirits, seeming to glide without legs.

"OK, party time, gather round," said Tighe. "This is how we'll play it. Douglas and Lambert, you take the tower sentries out after they change at midnight. Rogers and myself will deal with the patrolling guards and the vehicle park.

"Tinker Taylor and Daisy Green, you'll mine the living quarters and take out the radio operator *quietly*," he emphasized. "Cox and Winters, you open the main valves of the storage tanks and set two-hour fuses, but make sure you set the mines before you open the fuel valves. Get going. See you all back here in forty-five minutes. Set your watches and take care."

Jock Douglas and I approached the barbed-wire fence as close as possible, dropped into an irrigation ditch that ran around the outside of the camp, and lay there breathless, spending the next fifteen minutes watching the sentry walking slowly around the platform of the first watchtower.

"When we go in later," murmured Douglas as he worked his way to my shoulder, "you stick to me as though you were attached on your Mammy's right tit, if not closer. Don't want to lose touch with each other in the dark."

We poked our heads up above the rising mists to check on our quarry. I whispered, "He must get giddy, but it must be better than lying up to your cobblers in a muddy ditch."

However, it was the only camouflage for many yards, the jungle having been cut back to form a killing ground to deal with escapees and attackers. The machine gun emplacements dotted around the inside of the barbed-wire, when manned, made it a formidable challenge. It also straddled the approaches to the storage facilities, so all vestiges of opposition had to be removed before we could deal with the target.

After what seemed like an eternity of waiting for the guards to change, to allow themselves four hours of relative freedom, four guards accompanied by an NCO came marching towards us, rifles slung over their shoulders by the straps.

"Oh shite!" whispered Douglas. "The bastards have got a dog!"

Sure enough, the NCO was trying to control a big German Shepherd, who must have caught a slight scent of us as we tried to make ourselves invisible in the ditch. His only reward was a swift kick up the tail as his handler fought to get him under control.

"I was prepared to give him a dose from the crossbow," I said as I lowered my weapon after the crisis had passed. The crossbow was my weapon of choice; I preferred it, together with the knife, as being a guaranteed silent killer, which is why I suppose we had been picked for this particular little job.

The moon had risen and thrown everything into a stark relief, so we had to wait for the shadows of the tower to move over our positions in the ditch. This was the second time we had to wait for the vagaries of the moon before we could move. The first was to cover the crossing of the killing grounds where there was zero camouflage.

Halting at the base of the tower, a sentry detached himself from the detail, climbed up the swaying bamboo ladder on the inside of the structure, and disappeared through a trapdoor in the base of the platform. Shortly afterwards the relieved guard climbed down and fell in at the rear of the detail, and the party moved off.

Pushing the short crossbow in front of me, I wriggled the short distance to the bottom of the tower, followed by Douglas. We both knew that it must be a target of opportunity and that we must curb our impatience and wait.

Suddenly it presented itself; the sentry stopped and leaned his rifle against the parapet surrounding the platform, struck a match, and lit a cigarette. Cupping his hands to shield the glow he leaned on both elbows and gazed into the far distance, seeing nothing but the pictures of his own imagination. He drew contentedly on his cigarette, dragging the smoke deeply into his lungs, enjoying the final few moments of life that he was unaware he was about to lose. His head and shoulders were clearly defined above the parapet and his face illuminated as he repeatedly drew on his last smoke.

Placing the short bolt on the bow, I notched it into position and, taking careful aim, waited once more for the face to illuminate. As the smoke disappeared into his lungs, I fired.

Death was instantaneous; the bolt flew silently upwards, taking him beneath the chin and cleaving his tongue to the roof of his mouth as it travelled upwards to make its partial exit at the top of his head. The smoke that had been pent up in his lungs was released in one long sigh, and his knees buckled as he slowly sank to the platform.

"One down, three more to go, then we can go home," remarked Douglas.

The second tower had all the ingredients of a music hall farce. "It's as if they are waiting to come on stage," I murmured. "What's he doing now? I think he's taking a leak over the side. Well, I don't see how he can have a toilet up there and even he has to go somewhere, but I'll see if I can stop him."

The obliging moon had appeared and illuminated the sentry as he leaned with his back against the platform rails, throwing the upper part of his body into stark relief. Although no fine detail could be seen, he was sufficiently outlined to be a clean target.

Priming the crossbow once again, I raised it to my shoulder and gently squeezed the trigger. Once more, the harbinger of death flew silently upwards, but this time it struck the unfortunate guard at the base of the skull and made its partial exit through his left eye. He was dead before he started to fall forward and his momentum propelled him over the rail landing onto the ground with a sickening thud.

Two down, two to go. Too easy, but I think we'll accept it. It's time something went right. Now to the next one. Let's hope fortune keeps smiling, I thought as we made our way around the perimeter ditch that ran outside the barbed-wire. The only saving grace was that we had no open ground to traverse to the next tower; this coupled with the still swirling mist gave us plenty of cover.

"Hate to think what the hell we're crawling in," Douglas complained as he made his way on all fours behind me, pulling his elbows and knees out of the mud with a squelching sound that we were sure would be enough to waken the whole camp.

Arriving at the base of the third tower, we checked the time. The luminous face of the watch showed us to our amazement that it had only taken us twenty-four minutes, and we wondered how much longer our luck would hold out.

"I don't think he's going to oblige us by coming on stage to perform for us. He's probably got his head down, but don't rely on it. I'll keep the walkway covered while you climb up and give him his cue to come on stage."

Cutting the two bottom strands of barbed-wire we made our way beneath and wriggled through towards the inside of the tower.

"Wait until I reach the top of the ladder and then attract his attention away from the trapdoor," I whispered.

"What kind of noise do you want me to make, Jess?" Douglas queried.

"Don't give a monkey's. Bark like a dog, break wind, do anything to take his attention from the trapdoor."

The thirty-foot bamboo ladder swayed and complained alarmingly in the stillness of the night, and no matter how slowly I went up the rope lashings creaked at every movement, reminding me of an audience applauding an indifferent act.

Reaching the top of the ladder I was about to poke my head through the trapdoor in the floor to peer over, when suddenly, looking down at me in amazement and disbelief, there appeared a face, eyes round with surprise. His mouth started to open to shout a warning when my right hand shot up. Grasping him behind the neck as he lay looking down, I allowed my own weight to pull the sentry through the opening as I held on to the ladder with my other hand, and he spun over twice as he hurtled towards the ground. No need for Douglas to do anything when he landed beside him; the fall had broken his back and he joined his honourable ancestors without a murmur.

"Home from home up there," I said after climbing down the ladder. "Got a searchlight and telephone."

"So they need electricity, do they? So we'll find the cables and cut 'em off."

The next few minutes were spent in searching for the supply. We reasoned that it was likely to go up one of the supports, but the main supply could be left alone as no one would be up there to use it. The field telephone was a different kettle of fish. We could have problems if it rang and there was no one up there to answer it.

After peeling back the cable insulation, we cut one of the wires, hoping that the break in circuit wouldn't cause a bell to ring in the communication shack.

The last of the watchtowers was approached with greater caution; the open ground surrounding it made it a more formidable prospect. The ditch had petered out and the last of the natural cover disappeared more than forty yards short of the target. The mist, too, had begun to thin.

It was too far for an accurate bow shot and a bullet was too noisy. We lay side by side in the last of the sparse cover, bathed in sweat from our exertions and from the tension of the moment, tormented by a myriad of ants that patrolled these arid spaces searching for food, and that found the exposed flesh irresistible.

"I think we shall have to move from here, and damned quick or we'll be eaten alive. Let's try the bold approach and invite him down," whispered Douglas.

After waiting for an obliging moon to disappear behind a convenient cloud, we stood up, and with arms swinging we marched across the open space towards the tower, which seemed to get further away with every step. After what seemed an age, expecting to be challenged with every step we took, and desperately resisting the urge to run, we arrived beneath the cover of the tower, where we threw ourselves down thankfully and took a welcome breather.

"How do we invite him down? Better try knocking on the door, I suppose," said Douglas, answering himself. "Better get ready to introduce yourself, Jess, when he comes down."

Shrinking into the receding ground mist, he worked his way to the corner support of the tower. Drawing his revolver, he struck the upright three sharp blows with the butt end. It had to be repeated a further two times before there was any response from above. There was no mistaking the questioning tone directed to them below, which became more querulous as Douglas continued his rhythmic knocks. Unable to contain himself any longer the sentry lowered himself through the platform trap and began to climb down the swaying ladder.

With both hands occupied during his descent he was in no position to defend himself or offer any resistance when, waiting until he was almost to the ground, I reached through the rungs of the ladder. Gripping the unfortunate guard behind the head with both hands I pulled him forward, trapping his throat against the rung. The guard's whole weight was now supported on his chin as his arms and legs began to flail madly about. His eyes protruded as he fought for breath and the unequal struggle was brought to an abrupt end by a sudden jerk as his neck snapped with a sickening crack. The front of his pants suddenly darkened with wet staining and I gently lowered him to the ground with unexpected tenderness and compassion as I said, "Poor little bastard never stood a chance."

"Can't afford to give them a chance or it might be you lying down there, and just remember what happened to the Dakota pilot and his mate, and redirect your sympathy."

Now that the towers had been put out of commission, we gave the all clear signal to Sgt. Tighe and the team waiting in the deep scrub. They made their way across the killing ground and through the opening we had made in the barbed-wire fence, fanning out to their various targets.

Douglas and I attached ourselves to the oil storage team, rather than stand around like a couple of spare virgins at a wedding. Better to be active than wonder what was happening.

Tinker Taylor and Daisy Green, who had been surveying the layout of the compound, made their way to the long, low, heavily shuttered building and disappeared beneath its stilted structure.

A patrolling guard was strolling around with his rifle strung on his shoulder, with his mind probably at home in Nagasaki, when Green moved from the cover of the building and cut his throat from behind. Together they dragged him beneath the building. Now that any danger of being discovered for the time being had been eliminated they set about placing their time delays, one at either end of the building.

They were about to leave when a side door opened slowly, and they watched from the shadows as a half-dressed and emaciated figure swayed uncertainly down the steps, apparently to use the latrine bucket.

Looking at each other Taylor murmured to his mate, "What in God's name is that?"

"If I didn't know better I'd say it wasn't human," came the shocked reply.

Turning around, startled at the slight noise, the gaunt apparition, recognizing the two British soldiers, started to cry; sinking down on his knees and rocking himself to and fro he sobbed quietly and deeply, abandoning himself totally to his emotions.

Putting his arm gently around the man's shoulders, Taylor, with emotion almost as deep as the sobbing man's, chided him gently, "Come on, mate, you're all right now. We'll look after you."

Slowly the sobbing subsided, to be replaced by a wracking cough. "How many more of you are there?" Taylor asked quietly.

"Eleven," replied the bewildered man. "There were one hundred and thirty-six of us but we are the only ones left. The rest are buried outside the perimeter at the edge of the jungle."

The decision was made for them. "This puts a different complexion entirely on things," said Taylor decisively. "Go and find Sgt. Tighe down by the motor pool and fill him in with what's happened. I'll take it upon myself to get these prisoners outside the camp and deep enough into the jungle to be relatively safe."

When Green had left Taylor, he assisted the prisoner back up the steps, where they quietly wakened the rest of the sleeping men and readied them to leave.

The stinking barrack room seemed to ooze the fear and pain of every man who had ever been confined there. The stink was released by every movement of the men's feet as they walked across the floor, and erupted from the thread-bare blanket and rattan woven charpoys like some vile and evil essence.

"Answers will have to wait until later," Taylor told them in answer to a barrage of questions. "Suffice to say for the moment that we are not an invasive force, only a small party sent to do a particular job, but we'll take you out with us if you are willing to take the risk." With only a blanket and a mug to carry, they were virtually ready before he had finished speaking. "Don't worry about the guards. There won't be any around," he said.

Four of the prisoners were using makeshift crutches; one had to be carried and Taylor, being the only one strong enough, took him in a fireman's lift over his shoulder. Helping each other as best they could, they stumbled after Taylor, who led them to the cut wire fence and through into the jungle.

Finding what concealment they could after about half an hour they settled down for a brief rest and shared what little food Taylor had in his backpack. *If I had five loaves and two big fishes it wouldn't be half enough to feed these skeletons without divine intervention*, he thought irreverently.

"I thought I recognized an American and an Australian accent," he asked in some surprise.

"Yeah," replied a man with a deep Southern drawl. "We were all taken at the outbreak, separated from our wives and children, and have been in this hellhole ever since, watching our friends being carried out into the forest and wondering who the hell was going to be next. But one thing's for sure, I'm not going back into that hell again. Just give me a f-----g gun," he growled through the growth of a four-year beard.

"You won't have to, Yank," Taylor replied, "but save your energy for walking. We've got to put as much distance between the camp and ourselves as possible, so if you all think you are up to moving we have a rendezvous point to reach before first light."

Three years of deprivation and ill-treatment coupled with the inadequate food had taken its toll of the prisoners, but just to be outside the camp and free, however precarious their situation, gave them that injection of hope that in turn enabled them to dig deeply into a bank of reserves that was already very much overdrawn.

Looking back continuously at his new charges, Taylor marvelled at how they supported themselves on their fleshless spindles of legs, let alone motivated them to move. Ulcerated legs wrapped in filthy scraps of rag, badly swollen knee joints, and backs criss-crossed with wheals where their sadistic captors had beaten them with bamboo staves – all bore living testimony to Japanese depravity. These scarecrows, former managers, drillers, riggers and engineers employed by the oil company, whose knowledge and expertise had kept the oil flowing and the refineries at full pitch beneath the enemy's whips, were the pitiful remnants of a Western field force.

Nothing that the enemy did seemed to make any sense. They would beat and starve their workers to death and in consequence have to do progressively more for themselves. Their philosophy was that a prisoner of war was beneath contempt and was the lowest of the low. They considering themselves degraded even to be a guard in these situations. They could never accept the idea of being taken prisoner themselves, preferring death, in theory at least, rather than the stain of capture.

Guiding his little band deeper into the jungle Cpl. Taylor considered that the latter could well now have been arranged.

How they managed to cover the five miles back to the first rendezvous point was nothing short of miraculous. Carrying the weakest of the prisoners in turn, Taylor felt an overwhelming sense of guilt and pity at the remorseless pace he had to set. The alternative though was not even worth contemplating.

Finally, and in a state of complete exhaustion, they arrived at the secluded clearing and threw themselves down, too tired even to make themselves comfortable.

Taking off his backpack Taylor moved over to the Aussie, who had beckoned him. "Take a look, Corp," he murmured. "I don't like the look of a couple of them; I don't think they will be going any further."

Bending over a torn and dirty blanket, Taylor lifted it back and looked pityingly down at what had once been a man. With both legs drawn up under his chin, and with his thumb in his mouth in a womb-like position, he had died alone and quietly, using reserves he had dredged up from heaven knows where in gaining his freedom.

The figure beneath the second blanket was moaning quietly to himself, wracked with pain and clutching his stomach, talking to himself as if comforting a child.

"Who's Cathy?" Taylor asked the Yank, who had now moved over to join them.

"His little daughter. He was always taking about her. His wife died during the forced march to the camp."

Making a supreme effort in a final moment of clarity, the man opened his eyes, the sockets of which were black and deeply sunk. He lifted his hand to clutch the front of Taylor's shirt, and whispered so low that Taylor had to bend over him to hear. "Thanks, at least I didn't die in that hellhole."

Tears welled up in Taylor's eyes and his throat constricted with compassion. Quietly replacing the corner of the blanket he looked sadly across at the Aussie and shook his head. No need for words between them, and the glance had been interpreted by the rest of the exhausted party.

How many more would they lose before this caper was over? wondered Taylor, looking around. More than a hundred and twenty miles to go, over some of the worst terrain and conditions that could be imagined; hard enough if they were all in top shape, but this was nothing short of murder. All they really wanted was hospital nursing and attention. However, if none of them made it he was sure that he had done the right thing, and in the meantime, he had to make them comfortable.

Uncovering the personal packs, which had been deposited and hidden beneath the brush before the small party had moved out to carry out the attack at the camp, he undid them all, and committed the cardinal sin of violating someone else's kit. He took out the spare shirts, socks and shoes and distributed them to the half-naked men.

A man's personal kit was sacrosanct, but any explanations would have to wait until later.

Taylor lodged himself in the fork of a tree where he could look back down the track, and was satisfied that he had done all that he could. The rest was out of his hands, and now all he could do was watch and wait.

TWENTY

S GT. TIGHE, NOW JOINED BY DAISY GREEN, who had reported on finding the prisoners and the action already taken, were together cutting the fuel lines beneath the vehicles in the motor pool. They tackled the furthest away from the big storage tanks and worked their way towards the camp. Oblivious now of any noise they might make and secure in the knowledge that the two patrolling motor-pool guards would play no further part. With one being stabbed with his own bayonet after a short struggle, and his companion garrotted by Rogers with a long piece of metal flexible cord that he had withdrawn from his pesket (a special forces device, shaped like a sceptre at one end and used as a bludgeon). Pressing a button at the other end caused a sharp stabbing spike to spring out. This device was secured to the wrist by a canvas strip.

So positive had the guard's struggles been, and so violent, that his head had almost been severed. The dead guards' sightless eyes seemed to follow them around everywhere, and the feeling of being watched seemed unbearable, until in unison they went back and dragged their bodies into a convenient truck. *Must be going soft*, Tighe mused to himself, but felt distinctly better for it.

He glanced at his watch after digesting the changed circumstances and the problems caused by the release of the prisoners. The priority was not now merely the destruction of the camp and its facilities but the elimination of all possible pursuit.

Having to carry and help the former prisoners back was going to slow them down about 50 per cent. No more of the in and out undetected and the long delayed fuses, but the immediate elimination of even token opposition.

Tighe sent Rogers off to find the two Marines who had been detailed to mine the storage tanks, to acquaint them with the revised instructions to reduce the firing delay to forty minutes.

Having dealt with the vehicle park Tighe made his way to the nearest storage tank. Finding the flexible discharge pipes, he connected a line to the earthen embankment and turned on the main valve, looking back in satisfaction at the spreading fuel as it soaked the parched earth and slowly embraced each vehicle in a potentially lethal bath. The other tanks by now were spewing their deadly contents. Combining, the fuel began to encircle the buildings.

The blockhouse sentries had long ceased to have any interest in the proceedings, and to the casual onlooker seemed deep in conversation, leaning against the building, propped up by their rifles. Only the odd angles of their heads pointed to a more sinister reason.

The air was now heavy with lethal vapour and the need to move out became more pressing. *All it needs is some insomniac Nip to light a cigarette and we all fry together*, thought Tighe.

Looking at his watch, he realized that what had seemed an impossibility had been accomplished in a mere sixty-five minutes. Making our way to the perimeter wire we crawled through, and realizing that the new guard would be stirring pretty shortly, we virtually doubled to the edge of the jungle, where we threw ourselves down to take stock and regroup.

Our clothes were heavy with the smell of fuel and even at this distance, the air was oppressive and menacing. Still, moving away from the camp at the double it must have been twenty minutes before we stopped and checked our watches.

All eyes turned to the rear at the sound of a muffled explosion. Several others followed in rapid succession and the vehicle park, which by now had become a lake of fuel, suddenly ignited at both ends, and two arms of fire raced to meet each other and embrace the stationary trucks, which in turn added to the inferno as their tanks exploded and sent showers of sparks high into the air.

The blaze began sucking in air and superheating it in excess of two thousand degrees Fahrenheit, exploding it outwards in a tornado-force vortex.

Even at this distance, the exploding trees were showering hot embers down upon us like a swarm of angry bees, stinging any exposed flesh on arms or necks. The fine ash was so thick that we could taste the acrid grit upon our lips. Like an enraged monster, the twin arms of fire raced ahead, slashing through the short dry vegetation and howling with the towering sound of an express train.

The radio shack was the next to go up, and the operator, who must have been asleep, suddenly appeared in the doorway, his hair on fire. His face had erupted in one huge white blister, completely obliterating both his eyes. His mouth opened in a rictus of sound and he fell forward onto the ground enveloped in flames, screaming and rolling around, which only added to the inferno as the soaked earth ignited. He continued to scream until the pain and shock released him into oblivion.

The ammunition blockhouse caught, and the roof and sides disintegrated in one vast explosion followed by showers of tracer bullets that fanned through the night sky like some infernal fireworks display.

Shouts of alarm were filling the air as the Japanese soldiers began to pour from their sleeping quarters. Their voices turned to absolute terror as the enormity of their situation began to penetrate their sleep-befuddled minds and the arms of the flames began to embrace them.

No one could escape or survive a wall of fire that spread with such rapidity. The soldiers were trapped within this circle of death, which devoured their oxygen before igniting them and turning them into screaming balls of fire.

The big storage tanks were the next to ignite as one after another they exploded, shooting crimson tongues of flame hundreds of feet into the already glowing night sky and tossing waves of burning fuel over the camp and far into the encroaching jungle.

A stench of burning flesh began to pervade the air and the fire began to feed on itself, forming a vortex that spiralled hundreds of feet into the air. A huge pall of smoke formed over the whole area like some giant shroud.

Shaking his head in disbelief, Tighe murmured in an awed voice, "I can now say that I have been to the gates of hell, and if that's what it's like inside I'm going to change my ways, if it isn't too late. Come on, lads, there is nothing more we can do here."

The enormity of the devastation we had wreaked began to sink in. Nothing would remain in the area but blackened earth, nothing would survive that could be recognized. Perhaps in twenty or thirty years' time the jungle would advance to reclaim its own and cover the terrible scar when the soil had recovered its fertility, but at the moment the funeral pyre was still being fuelled by the millions of gallons of fuel oil and would probably burn for weeks.

Picking up our equipment in total silence, we stumbled in single file behind Tighe as he broke into a distance-eating trot.

The tall bamboo massed at the fringes of the foothills like a phalanx of Roman soldiers and just as impenetrable had to be detoured, and a deep penetration made towards the first rendezvous point where they expected to join up with Cpl. Taylor and his new charges.

The uninhibited approach of the returning attackers prompted Taylor to challenge and recognize his comrades, and the questions and answers that flowed to and fro between us and the former prisoners, with regard to the former guards, were amply illustrated by the orange glow that was visible far down the valley.

The general consensus amongst the former prisoners was that burning was far too good for the camp and guards, but the deed having been done, it was considered well done.

The ability of the prisoners to continue the march to the main rendezvous point didn't match their enthusiasm. In fact, for four of the worst cases it was decided to make litters of bamboo, and with the materials ready to hand it took no time at all. Despite protests from the four that were to be carried, it presented little or no problem as the weight of the heaviest one was no more than eighty pounds, considerably less than the loads that we had been packing when we started out.

Determined to put as much distance between ourselves and any possible pursuit, we decided to travel at night. Although our progress was much slower, it gave us satisfaction. Having decided this we picked up the litters, taking it in turns to share the additional carry, finding the easiest passage through the jungle rather than cutting and slashing, which would leave a trail for any pursuer to follow.

Dawn found us seven or eight miles into the jungle and at the prearranged rendezvous.

"Nothing to do now but to wait for the others," said Tighe. "Make your-selves comfortable; no sound, no smoke, which should be easy as we haven't anything to cook and all our fags are gone. Foremost though, make sure we do everything we can for our new charges. Whatever medicines or food we have, share them out between them. They are going to need all the strength we can give them when we start to move on again."

The rising sun began to dispel the ground mists and we found what comfort we could, sharing the last of the chlorinated water and hard biscuits. The little bits of chocolate and fruit that had been hoarded were collected and distributed amongst the ex-prisoners. We made them comfortable before turning in ourselves to snatch a few hours' sleep.

When the little group was roused towards morning by the guard, the four litter cases gave them all cause for concern, and it became clear that they were in the last stages of malaria. Mepacrine, quinine-based tablets, being a preventative not a curative, were too little too late, and all anyone could do was make them comfortable. Everyone felt helpless, watching the four alternately sweating and shivering, and prayed for them to let go of their tenuous hold on life to save them from further suffering.

It was midday, when the sun was at its most pitiless, that the last of the four died. They were buried side by side in shallow graves. The site was obscured by fallen forest timbers and brush, to prevent animal violation and to mask our escape route in the event of pursuit.

"No sign of the other team, Sarge," said Whitehouse. "How long do we have to wait for them?"

"We'll lie up for the rest of the day and then push on, whether or not they join us," Tighe replied, secretly feeling that they were now on their own. Something must have gone seriously wrong, perhaps caused by the premature blowing of the oil storage installation, but he had played the cards that had been dealt to him by fate the only way he knew. Any regrets he may have would have to be tempered by the care and wellbeing of his own men. Anyway, there was no going back.

He settled down with the rest of his men to await the return of the northern team, giving them every chance to catch up. We snatched what sleep we could from what was left of the day, as is the way of servicemen the world over, instinctively recharging our batteries against the time when a greater demand is made of us.

Lying on his back, his head cradled in the cups of his hands, Tighe looked up and through the canopy some two hundred feet or more above him, and marvelled at the upward thrust for light and life.

All the energies of the trees were used up in that essential drive for the light where they spread their branches, shutting out the sunlight to the dank, dark undergrowth below. The teeming life that they supported, brightly coloured birds, lizards, monkeys, snakes, never came down to the forest floor but spent their entire lives in the green tracery that provided them with food and security.

The only light that penetrated was by courtesy of one of these fallen giants that cut a swathe through the smaller trees and undergrowth as it fell, and even these monsters were soon swallowed up by the myriad of insects and fungi that eventually completed the cycle, returning the nutrients to the earth.

The vacated space in the canopy became a race for the lesser saplings to occupy, and the result was that scores of spindly plants would fail as they were elbowed aside in the upward thrust for light.

Gradually his eyes closed, but his mind went back, as it so often did during any appreciable lull. The past, it has often been said, is another country; if so, it is a place to which we have all travelled. We remember all its customs, we recall its highways and byways, we all know people there and we carry a passport and are citizens of that land.

A questing mind can transport a man to where he wants to be, lift him from where he is to do whatever he wants to do. Make him king for a day, captain of his own destiny, walking the lanes, making money or love.

It had all started with a Dear John letter waiting for him when he returned from a Gulf commission. An understanding CO and seventy-two hours' compassionate leave had seen him standing across the street opposite the little house he shared with his wife. As the letter had said, a car was parked outside!

He stood there watching the lights go out upstairs, his mind in a turmoil, until at breaking point he sprinted across the street, and without breaking stride put his shoulder to the door and raced upstairs, three at a time.

Unable to bluff it out the startled pair tried to separate, but could only do so with little dignity. Striding across the room Tighe raised the bottom sash window, then crossing to the bed he pulled the terrified man out by the scruff of the neck and one leg. He swung him once, then twice and propelled him through the open window.

With one long squeal, he somersaulted once and landed with a sickening thud on the top of his own car. Scrabbling in the boot, he sorted out the starting handle, and with swings of desperation managed to start it, all this only wearing a pyjama top. Dignity had been abandoned in the race for safety, and in his now badly dented Austin Ruby he thanked his lucky stars to have escaped relatively lightly.

Turning to his now crying, blustering wife, Tighe picked her up and carried her protesting downstairs, past the door, which by now was hanging off its hinges. He placed her on the pavement, still in her shortie nightie, into the night and the now pouring rain.

Turning his back on her, he went back into the house, climbed the stairs and threw her clothes through the window and into the street. All this without a word. Unable to control or trust his emotions and temper he sat down on the nearest chair, shaking and struggling to regain his composure.

What he had done had been in the heat of the moment. He was carried along on a wave of betrayal and hurt, but now that the action had passed and sanity was beginning to return he was thankful that he had had no weapon in his hand, or at least had not thought of using one. His eighteen-inch bayonet still hung from the frog on his belt, the vicious blade still safely contained in its scabbard, and he wondered what the outcome would have been if he had been aware of it.

During the commotion, lights had been switched on up and down the street. The neighbours had hung out of the upstairs windows to see the outcome of what had been inevitable.

The following day he re-hung the door, changed the locks, and gave all the furniture away. Leaving the house empty, he slammed the door behind him and returned the key to the landlord.

Walking back to the railway station with his kit bag on his shoulder he mentally wiped from his mind his childhood sweetheart and love of his life, his wife of two years and the very anchor of all his hopes and emotions.

She had known all about service life. Their courtship had been conducted by letter and the occasional leave so she had gone into marriage fully aware of the time spent apart, the enforced separations and the uncertainties of war. Perhaps she had been carried away by the other fellow's regular presence, the new car and expense account.

Thinking of money, when he got back to Plymouth he would stop all her allowances and set her adrift to paddle her own canoe. Thank his lucky stars he had found out, however much it hurt. In retrospect, he could only blame the war, the bloody war, and the loneliness of being apart. Yes, the war had a lot to answer for.

He was brought back to reality with a start, being shaken on the shoulder by Douglas saying, "Come on, Sarge, you've had a good four hours, and it's now fully dark."

We had already decided to travel only at night and to lie up during the day. As we had not been joined at the rendezvous point by Capt. Newsome and his team there was no point in hanging about. In fact, to do so might well have put us in some danger. Having heard sporadic bursts of gunfire to the north earlier, our general feeling was that the party had run into trouble. The firing had been repeated some time later, then followed by muffled explosions, which pointed to some success. However it wouldn't take the Japanese long to realise that there had been two separate operations against them, and they would be as angry as a hornet's nest poked with a long stick and would come looking.

To head for Cox's Bazaar, although forty miles further north and more difficult terrain, adding another three days to the journey, was thought to be less obvious and would possibly give us a day or two's start on our pursuers.

Our food was now all gone, having been shared with the ex-prisoners, but the last stop had provided us with full water bottles, which would have to be used sparingly.

We had ample ammunition; not a shot had been fired in anger. The accurate 303 LE Rifles had been left behind at base camp and traded for the tommy guns, weapons that could let you down in a tight spot by blocking, even though they had been carefully cleaned and wrapped in oilskins against the wet conditions.

This weapon care had been imprinted on us in far-off basic training, when we had learned to strip and reassemble them in the dark, each part being recognised by touch and caressed like an attentive lover. "Save your lives one day," the instructors had said. "Treat it as your best friend."

Preparing for the night's march became a ritual, each man suffering to varying degrees from prickly heat, dhobi rash, and the most debilitating of all, ringworm. The latter needed to be painted each day with gentian violet, a dye disinfectant used for treating burns and suchlike. Unlike the foo foo bird, as Denny Green quipped, these little parasites go round in ever-increasing circles.

The daily chore of painting each other's ringworm was made light of, and we likened this duty to a troop of chimps grooming each other to reinforce their family bonding.

Walking, too, became something of a nightmare. Each man suffered to varying degrees with jungle foot-rot, a kind of athlete's foot complaint that rotted the skin between the toes, leaving them cracked, painful and bleeding. Perhaps some Whitehall genius would some day catch on to the fact that the African divisions who fought alongside the Brits and who went mainly barefoot didn't suffer from it, and invent a boot (the design of which hadn't been changed since before the Boer War) that wasn't a sweatbox.

Ten minutes' rest every hour was a blessed relief from the back-chafing packs, and the opportunity to rest with your feet up was heaven, but the pain of starting off again made you wonder if it was worth it.

TWENTY-ONE

THE GROUND MISTS WERE BEGINNING TO LAY their ghostly shroud on the trail and the moon, now in full radiance, promised another night's march. The sounds of the day had given way to a clamorous night shift. The trumpeting of the wild elephants formed the bassoon backing of the nocturnal orchestra, the incessant fluttering of the pigeons and parrots as they changed their perches in the high canopy. As long as you recognized that the grunts, squeals, and sudden silences were the natural accompaniments to jungle living, and not man-made, it was not complacency, but a ready acceptance of a greater order of things, that enabled you to rationalize jungle existence and keep it in some kind of perspective.

Dawn was beginning to break when we appeared to be approaching some form of habitation, betrayed by the smell of wood smoke. We proceeded with heightened caution, sure that we would be betrayed by the village dogs. Breaking day revealed a compound of about twenty *bashas*, stilted low bungalows raised to combat the onset of the monsoon rains. Our caution was fully justified, for flying over the largest of the dwellings was the flag of the rising sun.

Five o'clock was too early for anyone to be about, so the main party concealed themselves in the surrounding cover whilst Sgt. Tighe and Denny Green crawled their way beneath the nearest of the huts. Covered by Green, Tighe made his way cautiously up the steps and pushed open the light bamboo door. Fully awake and cowering in the corner, the six occupants regarded him with some amazement.

After the first muted excitement had died down, Tighe managed to discover, through signs and broken English, that the Japanese had been in the village for about two months, had taken the headman's family hostage against the village's

110

cooperation and good behaviour, and were systematically eating them out of house and home.

The young women had managed to escape into the jungle, but there had been executions, and four bodies had been left hanging at the far end of the village for all to see.

"A sergeant and nine men shouldn't prove too much of a problem," remarked Tighe later when everyone had been put in the picture. "Especially as they aren't expecting anyone. They must feel pretty secure in the one hut and no sentries out."

"How shall we do it, Sarge? Light a fire under them and pick them off when they come out?" was the general comment.

"No, too noisy, gunfire would be heard for miles and would be recognised as British fire, and would alert every Jap in the area."

The Yank and Aussie had begged to be allowed to take part in the cull and were given the use of knives, but under supervision. It was generally felt that it was some kind of poetic justice. Approaching the long, low buildings in the cover of the rapidly shortening shadows, Douglas and Green quietly ascended the steps and entered the darkened room.

The sickly, sweet smell common to all Japanese soldiers filled the air, and the snores and grunts of the sleeping men muffled any small sound Douglas and Green made as they threaded their way between the two rows of beds to take up position where they could cover both sides of the room. They crouched in the deep shadows, waiting for their eyes to become accustomed to the stinking room.

After what seemed an eternity, they became aware of movement in the room as Sgt. Tighe and the rest went about their deadly business. The last to be dispatched was the Jap sergeant, who was lying on his side, asleep, with his arm flung over a terrified native girl who had witnessed the whole proceedings with wide frightened eyes, mercifully too afraid to make a sound. Motioning the girl to remain silent Tighe dispatched him and released her from his instinctively tightening embrace.

Picking up her clothes the girl ran out of the room and fled headlong down the steps, soon to be surrounded by vocal and excited villagers. Soon, however, their joy gave rise to concern as the reality of what had taken place began to dawn on them, and the fact that this was not an army of liberation, but the remnants of a tired little force struggling back to their own lines.

As they were fearful of reprisals from the retreating Japanese when the small British force left, it was decided to conceal their occupation. Tighe reasoned that without wireless contact it could only have been a rogue detachment taking advantage of a village situation without fear of opposition, so perhaps no one would miss them.

For the villagers the rice planting season was in full swing and the availability of an unplanted paddy field suggested an obvious solution. Setting to with goodwill, the natives dug a large hole in the centre of the field whilst the Brits cleaned up the camp, carrying the wrapped corpses and placing them at the bottom of the excavation.

Weighting them down with heavy stones, we puddled them in with clay that had been dug out of the riverbed. "Like treading grapes," said Stan Whitehouse as he squelched his feet out of the clay. "Only this is one vintage we don't want uncorking."

Flooding the field when the levelling mud had covered everything effectively obliterated any trace that could compromise the village, and we expressed ourselves satisfied that everything that could be done had been done.

The females, who had returned from their hiding place in the jungle meanwhile, had been preparing food, and judging from the smells that pervaded the whole village it promised well.

Settling down with our hosts we soon realised that the few remaining chickens had been killed to provide what to the villagers was a feast; such was their appreciation and goodwill. The chicken was served on a bed of rice in a wooden bowl, followed by freshwater shrimps and fish.

At another time and in other circumstances, the setting would have been better appreciated. Even so, the idyllic surroundings were not lost on any of us. All around grew areas of fruit trees, mango and tamarind, which were shaded by rows of giant ferns.

Towering above them all were the coconut palms, banyan and toddy plants. The latter when fermented produced a delicious alcoholic drink, which gave the word 'toddy' to the British vocabulary.

It quickly became apparent that these people were virtually self-sufficient, happy to be left alone and not burdened with what we take for granted as necessities.

Cascading over everything and drenching the air was the honey-sweet smell of jasmine, 'queen of the night'. Not even the reality of war could detract from the natural beauty and delights of nature, the sudden darting of the brightly coloured birds and the unbelievably decorated butterflies that seemed to hover like kites before settling to feed on the descending folds of hibiscus.

With the meal, the shrill chorus of the innumerable cicadas formed an extempore orchestral accompaniment heightening the bizarre situation, lulling us into a false sense of security and wellbeing.

This idyllic interlude, however, had to end sooner rather than later, and to make sure that the village wasn't compromised we toured around with the headman until he was satisfied that all traces of the Japanese occupation had been eliminated.

The water level of the newly flooded paddy field and the levelling mud beneath had concealed what secrets were buried there. The rising sun flag had been taken down and presented to Sgt. Tighe, who folded it up and put it into his pack as a souvenir.

Fully satisfied, the headman conveyed his thanks to us all, and reluctantly we said our goodbyes to a very friendly and happy village.

Our packs had been replenished with fruit, particularly tamarind. This fruit wouldn't rot; in fact, it is better dry, like pea pods. Although composed of ball-bearing-like seeds, the flesh is sweet and nutritious.

Gathering our belongings together we looked back occasionally until we were out of sight and in the fringes of the jungle.

The night was suddenly cold and black as pitch and the only progress we could make at all was by clinging to the backpack or bayonet scabbard of the man in front for fear of losing contact.

Suddenly and without preamble a huge moon topped the An ridge and bathed everything in its brilliance. Its clear light played amongst the trees so that they seemed to have queer shapes moving about them.

Progress was becoming more difficult and although we were following a small tributary this could and probably would discharge into one of the many *chaung*s that criss-crossed the land. The undergrowth was such that it was necessary to take the lead in turns to cut a way through. Half an hour was sufficient for the lead to be left with blistered hands and a sweat-soaked shirt; what made things worse, the sleeves that hung down from the brim of the bush hat over the face restricted vision and clung to the face, making it sweaty and uncomfortable.

When we were far enough away from the village it became necessary for us to conceal our tracks, and we decided to construct booby traps of Japanese hand grenades that had been collected and packed away with their own kit. To lay traps with British grenades would point to our presence and again compromise the village. This should slow down any pursuit, using the natural vines as tripwires; these would decay in about five weeks, and should only be effective against immediate attack.

Satisfied that we had taken all possible precautions we continued our push throughout the night.

TWENTY-TWO

C APT. NEWSOME LED HIS PARTY INTO THE gathering gloom and quickly disappeared from sight, confident of his own and Sgt. Tighe's ability to accomplish their missions.

The more northern team had about seven miles to go, but with timing of the essence, both attacks had to go in at the same time to ensure maximum success. This would then allow a more planned withdrawal.

Working by compass, the cut and slash direct route was proving the most satisfactory. To search for worn and travelled pathways could only lead to discovery, besides being time-consuming. With one eye on the clock they took the lead in turns, wielding the big *pangas* to maximise efficiency.

Suddenly the two forward scouts signalled for silence and camouflage, and the following file of men responded by falling flat at the side of the track, squirming their way into the encroaching scrub.

Hardly daring to breathe they watched as a Japanese patrol filed past with rifles slung, chattering and laughing and completely at ease.

"I counted twelve," said Cookie. "Pity we couldn't have taken them out. It would have been all the less to do later."

"Too much noise, too near the camp. We can't afford to compromise the operation. Anyway, they are probably going back to camp to get their heads down, and we can always give them a visit before we pull out," replied his oppo, Howard.

A few minutes later on, they decided it was an isolated patrol and that it was safe enough to use the track again. No more cut and slash, but they still set the forward scouts. No unpleasant surprises that way.

The lightly worn track was no gentle walk in the forest, and whilst speed was essential, it was not secondary to safety. Anything out of the ordinary had to be treated with extreme caution. Bushcraft took pride of place in all their training. Grasses bent the wrong way, twigs and leaves broken were all pointers that had to be interpreted and explained.

The forward scouts certainly earned their pay when they held up their hands to warn for caution. A tripwire stretched across the track was only discovered at the last minute. Motioned to come forward, the Captain took the situation in at a glance. After casting around for a long stick he pushed at the tripwire, which in turn released a spring-loaded trap, which slammed a six-foot bamboo structure across the track, burying the sharpened stakes deep into the trunk of a tree. Anyone taking the brunt of this device would suffer a hideous end.

Further along, the scouts discovered deep pits, the bottom of which had been planted with sharpened bamboo stakes. The points had been smeared with disgusting rubbish, mainly excrement. If the stakes didn't kill you the infection certainly would.

All this increased protection pointed to the fact that they must be approaching the site.

Their first task was to find the communication shack, which was usually situated a little apart from the main camp for security reasons.

With tommy guns at the ready, safety catches off, they filed in complete silence. They were fully aware of the time schedule and the need for an insertion coordinated with Sgt. Tighe's operation on the other target, in order to mitigate any potential cock-ups and to maximise the element of complete surprise. The priority was to find the radio shack and take it out without raising any alarm that could jeopardise both operations.

After some short time the forward scouts reported sighting an isolated low building with two radio masts. The pale lantern light that spilled from the unshuttered windows clearly pointed to someone being at home and awake.

A single patrolling sentry with rifle slung was dreaming along with his head wreathed in a cloud of black smoke, oblivious to the world around him, when Howard was given the nod to deal with him.

Don't look around, thought Howard as he approached him in the shadows from behind. Picking his aiming spot he suddenly lunged at him with the stabbing spike of his special forces pesket, driving it beneath his helmet and up into his brain. The silence was unbroken, and Howard caught the sentry as he fell and rolled him off the side track into the low scrub.

He signalled back to the Captain, who took it as his cue to join Howard. Together they made their way to the isolated shack whilst the rest of the team remained in camouflage to await the outcome, fully alert and covering them both in case of discovery.

Cooke took up his position to cover the doorway as his two comrades approached the unshuttered windows at the rear. Peering cautiously over the sill they saw the radio operator leaning back in his chair in front of his brightly illuminated dials, earphones clamped onto his head and a laryngaphone (throat microphone) around his neck, obviously on duty watch. His companion was busy making a brew on the table-top stove, and both of their attentions were completed absorbed.

Motioning to Howard, the Captain drew his revolver and screwed the silencer into place. He noted that his companion was doing the same. They rested their firearms on the low sill. The revolvers coughed in unison, twice. Just two taps, as in training; once was never considered enough. Putting a shot between the eyes was reserved for the movies and John Wayne. Just two taps into the largest target, the chest, was usually more than enough and safer.

Entering the shack through the windows they secured the radio operator in his chair in front of his set, before smashing sufficient valves to render the set useless. The char maker was laid down on his truckle bed, as if asleep.

Collecting what remnants of food they considered palatable, the Captain and Howard closed the door. Returning to the waiting squad they shared out the pieces of bread, cheese and fruit. They considered that they had about two hours before the radio operator was due to be relieved. That should leave them plenty of time to get in and out.

They were beginning to glimpse, between the trees, the perimeter lights that marked the installations' enclosure, and shortly after they were in sight of the production rigs, drill heads and extensive crude oil storage facility that they had come so far to destroy.

Realising the target was too brightly illuminated for them to attack with safety, the Captain detailed two marines to find the generators and put them out of action, and they all had to be patient again whilst they waited for the lights to go out.

Identifying the main generator and the back-up as being the smaller of the series, the two marines removed the oil filler caps and poured in handfuls of sand scooped up from the parched ground. This would look to be a normal mechanical breakdown and would take a little time to find and longer to put right, by which time they hoped to be gone. Far better than giving their presence away by blowing up the generators or shooting out the lights.

They didn't have to wait long for the generators to start to cough and miss. After a few minutes, the perimeter lights faded out.

There was nothing to indicate to the Japanese technicians the nature of the failure. Both main and back-up generators were down, and they could be seen examining the motors with torches that flashed alternately between them and the pylons.

Blessed darkness had descended and the saboteurs joined their comrades for the next phase. They lay up, camouflaged in the low scrub that petered out some few yards before the perimeter wire, weighing up the layout and planning their attack. A time-delayed limpet mine was more than sufficient to destroy the nodding jennies. These effectively set them on fire, making it virtually impossible for them to be put out and capped without the specialised personnel and equipment.

Without this expertise to hand, the means of production and storage were denied to the Japanese and would make their retreat down one of the few metalled roads to Rangoon impossible. There would be insufficient fuel for the boats to enable them to do a Dunkirk down the Irrawaddi, so they would have to stand and fight.

The production fields were patrolled by roaming sentries, who appeared to keep no set pattern but passed each other in pairs, stopping to smoke and chat when they met.

Lying in the light cover the attacking team waited for the prearranged time, which passed fifteen minutes before the guards changed; fifteen minutes that were going to have dire consequences before the night was over.

Each man carried four time fuse-activated mines, and it was decided to work in pairs, one to lay and set and the other to stand guard over him. Waiting for the sentries to change, and knowing that they had a full twenty minutes before they passed again, the team cut the perimeter wire and crawled through. Running between the shadows cast by the storage tanks and the oil pumps they went to work with some haste, setting and concealing the mines with two-hour fuses, calculated to give them ample time to finish the job and get well clear.

With each rig being taken in sequence, and then the big crude oil storage tanks being attended to, everything was going like clockwork, just like a session in training, and they were getting ready to withdraw.

Suddenly the sky lightened, and from some ten miles away it took on an unnatural orange glow, followed seconds later by ear-shattering explosions. Five more minutes and they would have all withdrawn from the site, but suddenly the buildings that flanked the southern end of the oilfield disgorged curious and alarmed guards.

Marines Howard and Cooke had already laid their mines, retired through the perimeter wire, and made their way into the surrounding cover where they lay camouflaged, waiting for the rest of the team to join them.

"Looks as though the lads are going to be cut off," said Marine Howard. "Although the Nips don't know we're amongst them yet. We can't leave them in there on their own. Let's go back in there and give the Japs a couple of grenades to draw their fire so the lads can get out."

Without hesitation and fully aware of the risks they were taking Howard and Cooke made their way back to the cut perimeter wire.

"On my count of three. Pin, two, three."

The two grenades curved an arc and landed amongst the curious Japs. No one realised what was happening until they exploded, cutting down the middle section and leading edge of the milling men, by which time the second and third grenades had been released. The twin explosions decimated the remaining men who hadn't flung themselves flat. The remnants were crawling away to find what cover they could before taking up a defensive stand and preparing to fight back.

The enemy, now realising which quarter the attack was coming from, were beginning to spread out and flank the diversionary attack. Howard's and Cooke's position was now becoming untenable, but it had only been taken up in the first place to allow their comrades the chance to withdraw, which became less and less possible as they were being pressed on three sides. With only two grenades left, they decided to use their tommy guns, taking it in turns to pick off, on single shot, the attackers and to conserve ammunition.

Howard had taken a hit in the right lung and was now leaning against the bole of a tree. He was breathing with great difficulty and fighting to focus his eyes, the lids of which seemed to have minds of their own and were doing their best to shut. Howard looked towards his mate and in a shallow voice said, "Leave me here, Cookie. I'll cover you. Get out when you can."

"Not on your life," replied his mate. "We came in here together and we'll leave together. Or not...." The last words he murmured under his breath.

The ammo was now all gone. "Time for grenades," they said in unison – the time-honoured exit. Drawing the pins and throwing them far away, they kept both grenades tightly held to retain the springs, and waited.

The Japanese soldiers, probably realising that the two were out of ammunition, suddenly became brave. They stood up and began to advance on the two men from three sides, probably dreaming of medals, displaying boldness that replaced caution, seeing that they were not armed. They brought down their rifles from the high port to point their bayonets threateningly, and looked fully intent on using them.

In the time-honoured manner Howard and Cooke both said, "See you in Hell!" and released the pressure on the spring clips. Timing their throws to perfection, they gently lobbed them into the advancing semi-circle, where they exploded virtually on contact and cut a vicious swathe through the enemy.

Whatever time Howard and Cooke had hoped to buy for their comrades had now been paid for in full, and when their position was overrun they became planned casualties of their own grenades.

Seeing the glow in the distance, Capt. Newsome realised that Tighe had set off his charges before the agreed time for whatever reason, and now that the mines had been set on their targets they had no more reason to hang about.

The firing that was coming from the perimeter, he realised, was being laid down to cover his team's withdrawal, but with the enemy now fanning out and the support fire now silent he reckoned he was on his own.

A big searchlight had been switched on and the enemy advanced in line, sweeping the site for any other intruders. There was to be no escape. The perimeter lights had also been switched on full, illuminating everything like day, revealing in stark relief the five remaining Marines, who were doing their best to remain concealed.

A short burst from a tommy gun extinguished the searchlight and killed the two operators, but there was still sufficient light for the Nips to home in on their quarry. Then from the shadows, a heavy machine gun kicked up puffs of dust around the prone forms of the attacking team, who had taken shelter in the folds of the ground.

"If we stay here any longer we're going to be picked off one by one without being able to reply," shouted the Captain. "Let's go and meet them and take a few with us."

To their eternal credit, no one spoke of putting their hands up, fully accepting the outcome of their proposed actions. To fall into the hands of the Japanese as prisoners was unthinkable. Their bestiality was legendary; the Geneva Conventions merely a fairy story. Best to go out cleanly.

Waiting until the advancing line of soldiers were within thirty yards, they stood up and launched the last of their grenades at them. Then with tommy guns blazing they walked towards the enemy, cutting down those in their path.

There could only be one outcome; the odds against survival were nil. When their magazines were empty they drew their revolvers and continued to fire until one by one they fell beneath the murderous crossfire laid down upon them.

Barely one hour later, the reason for their attack became all too apparent. The Japanese, believing that they had prevented any damage to the installation, suddenly found themselves in the middle of an inferno as one by one the oil rigs erupted in a frenzy of flames. The ruptured pumps and pipes spewing burning tar-like oil a hundred feet into the air, and the well-heads, under continuous pressure and alight, roared into the air like giant blowtorches.

The containers of crude oil awaiting dispatch to the nearby refinery suddenly disintegrated, their contents spewing out onto the already soaked earth, where they ignited, spreading the flames to the living quarters and storerooms of the Japanese garrison.

The fallen Marines, together with the bodies of their enemies, became part of the funeral pyre. Later, if there was to be any recovery, there would be nothing to differentiate one from the other.

The Japanese, without the knowledge or capacity to extinguish the fires and to subsequently cap them would leave them burning, producing an enveloping black cloud hovering like a shroud over the entire valley.

TWENTY-THREE

THE FIRST MORTAR BOMB FELL ABOUT THIRTY yards ahead of the resting Marines. The next two bracketed us left and right, galvanizing us into instant action. The fourth, fifth, and sixth fell simultaneously amongst the milling men, and the effect was instant and appalling.

The trees surrounding the clearing where we had been resting suddenly became an obscene gallery, displaying the remnants of what had been, until moments earlier, two men. Pieces of clothing, tufts of hair, entrails and strips of flesh hung from the lower branches of the trees, whilst the leaves and trunks that formed the walls of this nightmare gallery had been repainted in red as if from a madman's palette.

Two hands, which the survivors took to be those of Bob Rogers because of the signet ring, still gripped a tommy gun, the right index finger curled around the trigger as if awaiting the order to fire.

The hands, however, were attached to nothing. The bodies that had motivated them, had been shuffled, like some giant jigsaw, but with the pieces so scattered, and so many missing, that only a divine hand could complete the picture.

The two heads, which miraculously had remained intact, had rolled to the edge of the scrub, and with wide-open eyes they seemed to survey each other and the surrounding carnage with concern and disbelief.

The three stretcher cases, who had been carried for most of the journey and who had been resting beneath the shade of a large banyan tree, had also taken the full spread of shrapnel and would tragically no longer be the responsibility of the carrying party.

Their makeshift stretchers, which had been cobbled together from bamboo and spare webbing, would now form the top section of a shroud that had to be hastily thrown over them because of the urgent need to get moving and to avoid contact with a much superior force.

"Unless you want to join 'em, shift your arses. Nothing more we can do here," yelled Tighe.

Needing no further bidding, and his order being underlined by further mortar bursts, luckily not on target, the diminished party hastily picked up our equipment, and following the Sergeant's lead we topped the rise and stepped into a dry watercourse, slipping and stumbling on the moss-covered stones.

The mind plays funny tricks during times of stress. Denny Green, hastily collecting his kit, suddenly had visions of Bob Rogers' wife lying on the edge of the big double bed with her knees drawn up, gripping the rear hem of her nightgown under her chin in an attitude of silent self-defence. *No need to any more*, he thought, *now you will be able to luxuriate in your own company and spend the rest of your nights, lonely, in the middle of the bed.*

Is this what it was going to be like then, knowing nothing, wiped out in the twinkling of an eye? Still, better this way than lying rotting in bed, being eaten from the inside by some unspeakable disease. No one was exempt; we all have to go sometime; the how, the where and the when being the great imponderables. This was the only philosophy he could subscribe to. Being fatalistic, he could accept the idea of being killed, but not of being wounded and helpless.

There is a randomness about death that most people find repellent. If there was one that had your name on it, you would have to accept it. It was the one addressed *to whom it may concern* that was the worry; the indiscriminate.

Shaking himself mentally, he finished picking up his gear and followed the rest of the party, who were disappearing over the rise.

Tighe reasoned that the watercourse should lead to the valley floor, and by the easiest available route, although it could also work against them. Finding no tracks the pursuers would guess that this was the only route they could have followed. With this in mind, he led his diminished party out of the dry streambed and into the jungle. After about two miles, we doubled back and continued our course.

All depends how astute the Japs are, Tighe thought. *If it was me I would split my force up at this point. Still, the subterfuge might give us half a day's lead.* Already in his mind he was contemplating the confusion that would be caused if they could reach the comparative safety of the trail back over the An Pass, where their pursuers would run into their own retreating forces.

Knowing that the Nips were coming up behind us, more cautiously perhaps, but still as relentless, gave us all the spur we needed. With the height of the scrub and wandering nature of the stream screening us from any searching eyes we plunged downhill at breakneck speed, oblivious of any noise, just feeling the desire to put as much distance between ourselves and our pursuers as possible.

The alternative strategy of leaving the dry watercourse, concealing ourselves and allowing the Nips to go by had already been dismissed as not on by Tighe. He reasoned that the Japanese would realise what had happened and eventually double back to carry out a more exhaustive search, making our position indefensible.

Calling a halt to what seemed like hours of descent, Tighe looked around at the remaining seven Marines and the Yank and Aussie camp survivors and marvelled at what he saw. They were wet through, with clothes torn to shreds, unshaven, bleeding from a multitude of falls and vicious thorn bushes, yet they would still follow him unquestioningly, and he for his part would be proud to lead them.

After a break of about fifteen minutes we needed no persuading to get up and to start moving again, being aware of what was coming up behind us. Although every instinct was to stand and fight this was neither the time nor the place. If we had to stand it would be somewhere of our own choosing, where we had some chance and could inflict the greatest number of casualties.

During our descent to the valley floor, we paused occasionally to listen for sounds of pursuit. Although the jungle was neutral and provided us with sufficient cover to cloak our retreat it could also provide an enemy, whichever quarter he came from, with the same service.

The streambed, however, which for so long had masked the way of our passing, was beginning to search for a different course, which would ultimately take it by some tortuous route to discharge into the Irrawaddi River, where we had just come from. It was therefore time to part company, with darkness almost upon us. The necessity of covering up signs of our passing meant that we were forced to spend an uncomfortable night in a large outcrop of rocks.

There was no need to post any sentries. The bullfrogs, whose raucous chorus would continue until daylight, were all we needed. The cacophony of sound would cease as if directed by an orchestral baton if any unnatural sound was heard, however stealthy.

The flaming ball of the sun was beginning to announce its rising, and one by one the bullfrog croaks ceased as they sank beneath the black alluvial mud that still retained some moisture along the banks of the dry streambed.

We stretched, scratched, cursed, stood up, put our packs on, and looked around to see Tighe, who by this time was striding towards the edge of the jungle, drinking from his bottle as he went.

TWENTY-FOUR

Pausing occasionally to refer to his compass, Sgt. Tighe set a relentless pace, fully intent on putting as much distance as possible between us and our night camp, intending to cut the An track through the saddle pass at the first opportunity.

Whitehouse, whose stomach wound was causing him to lag behind, could see the tail end of the column receding in the distance. Although the wound had stopped bleeding as severely as before he could still detect the telltale steady trickle that caused his trouser leg first to wet and then to stiffen.

Tightening his waist belt up a couple of notches had temporarily relieved the pain but he suspected that the blood he wasn't seeing was collecting internally, and the feelings of dizziness were now becoming more frequent.

The midday break allowed him to catch up with his comrades, who had divvied up the small amount of fruit and berries that we had been collecting during our march and were now lying around in various stages of rest and exhaustion.

Lowering himself down gingerly he said, "I think you're going to have to go ahead without me, Sarge, I picked up a bit of shrapnel when we were mortared."

"Why the hell didn't you open your face before?" Tighe replied. "No use you being a bloody hero. Let's have a look." Undoing Whitehouse's belt and shirt, Tighe looked at the small blue hole at the bottom of the stomach, which suddenly blossomed again when the pressure was released. "I hate bloody heroes. You can't walk any further with this." Turning to the rest of the party, who by this time had gathered around, he said, "Cut enough material for a stretcher. We've got some carrying to do."

Tighe made a pad out of his last spare shirt, and using the belt again for pressure, strapped Whitehouse up again. He gave him the last of the water from his own bottle; the wrong thing to do with a stomach wound, but what the hell, it wasn't going to make any difference. Might as well make him as comfortable as possible for the short time he had left. This kind of wound didn't get better by being wrapped up. What Whitehouse needed was a hospital and a surgeon, but there was no chance of that, and the four or five days back to base was going to be too many.

The fact that he had got this far was nothing short of miraculous, but we were prepared to carry him for long as it took. Any first aid that we could manage was only the sticking plaster variety. The ampoules of morphine and sulphur powder had been exhausted by the prisoners we had rescued, and the only one with any medical knowledge at all had gone with Capt. Newsome's party.

Whitehouse, whose face by this time was twisted in pain, stared at Tighe, then looked away. "I've got a notion to stay right here, Sarge. I'm sure I can't make it any further."

"You'll make it all right or I'll want to know the reason why. No use you wasting all this effort and steps you've already taken to get here."

No doubting Tighe; he made everything seem possible, thought Whitehouse. Certainly a man of definite mind, strong and positive in his opinions, he approached every problem with a certainty that there could be just two possibilities – his own way, and the wrong way. The opinions he expressed had been taken on board with his mother's milk and nothing he had subsequently experienced had served to change any one of them. So positive was he in his leadership that his men followed him without question, knowing that any decision he made would be the right one, taken only after weighing up all the odds.

The sounds of the jungle are small sounds, sounds and small noises that the ears must become attuned to if one is to survive. In a man, when required, there lie deeply embedded the remains of the primitive, and after a while his senses become more acute and accustomed to nature. However, he must listen well; he must wait and give himself time to become attuned to the wavelength of the jungle and to be aware of the things around him.

Jungle fighting is a series of close, quick encounters, where a man's life hangs on his own foresight and cunning, coupled with his own alertness, speed and skill. More often than not you are out of touch with a platoon commander, or even a patrol leader. Individual initiative is essential and must be decisive. Man is opposed to man.

At midday, with it being the stifling period just before the monsoon and with temperatures reaching some 120 degrees, nerves were on edge and tempers at breaking point waiting for the massed storm clouds to break and bring blessed relief from the intolerable sultriness.

Clean drinking water in abundance – the thought of it caused Tighe's mouth to salivate around the small stone that he was sucking. Looking at the mountain ranges that flanked the valley, he saw that they were rocky ridges, sharp and clear against the sky. He tried to estimate the distance. Five miles? Ten? No, closer to twenty, but before then they should cross the track to cut through the saddle pass back over the An Range.

The heat did not seem to lessen as the afternoon wore on, and the stretcher party, who had been alternating, were slowing down now to a mere walk. We were relieved to find a stand of bamboo, some of which were the thickness of a man's thigh and which the natives used as buckets and storage containers by cutting it off below one of the joints. Splitting the smallest of these, we tapped into a fresh supply of water, enough to slake our thirsts and fill our water bottles.

The afternoon was drawing to its close and the distant shapes of the Arakan Yoma had adorned themselves with the rosy hue of impending sunset. The abrupt and sheer cliffs that flanked the saddle pass, lifting some half a mile above the valley floor, had adopted the dappled sheen conjured up by the failing light, giving the whole of the distant aspect the inviting and welcoming appearance of rest and coolness.

It was probably all an illusion, though. Close at hand we would be subjected to the same remorseless battering of the sun.

Suddenly and without further preamble darkness pounced like some thief in the night to steal without thought the light from the day and somehow reflect it back as a pale luminary, giving the jungle giants the appearance and frightening aspect of evil.

It had become cold, the clammy cold of the jungle night. The residue of the daytime heat had dissipated, leaving a cold that penetrated through the thin clothes of those who travel dressed only for the excessive heat of the day.

Having called a halt, we settled down for the night, and Tighe set two-hourly watches, taking the first himself. Sweat still accumulated on him and dripped from his face, and it surprised him that there was so much moisture remaining in his body.

His lips were sunburnt and cracked and his eyes smarted from sun-scoured rims. *Still, we are all the same*, he thought, so like the rest of them he'd grin and bear it. Didn't have to like it, though.

Looking around him at the sleeping men, he studied each one closely. Yank and Oz looked to be at the end of their tethers, and he marvelled that they had come so far. They might want a ride come morning. Still, they must move on, for their pursuers were still vengeful and persistent, and nothing short of death would dissuade them.

At the end of his watch he was relieved by Douglas. Exchanging curt pleasantries Tighe made his way to the two large trees he had already selected and lowered his weary frame into the hollows provided by the trees' sprawling roots. Knowing the watch was in capable hands he shut his eyes. Sleep came as it often did to exhausted men, instantly but shallow, and he awoke often, as was his habit, listening for a few moments, then sleeping again.

It made no difference that someone was reliable and on watch, and it was no reflection on their capabilities, but he had survived so long in such places as this, where to sleep too soundly might invite death, and he had lost the habit of sleeping through the night with an untroubled mind.

The disturbance some half a day's march behind them indicated that their pursuers had not given up, but on the contrary had made some significant effort to close the gap. Whitehouse, who was complaining more and more every time he was moved, begged Tighe and the others to leave him behind the next morning as he realised that he was responsible for their lack of progress.

"Leave me at the side of the trail, Sarge," he said. "With a couple of clips of ammo I'll get you some more time, and take some of the little bastards as company. I think I owe them one."

Tighe had seen so many people die, a lot without the dignity that they deserved when death had marked them down, but Whitehead had chosen, and chosen well. There was no better way to meet death than face to face, and no better way to die than to die a Marine.

Reluctantly we, his comrades, packed our equipment, and despite the protests of the carrying party and the rest of us, he was made as comfortable as possible at the base of one of the largest trees with the last bottle of water at his side.

Waving as his companions disappeared out of sight he settled himself down, unable to smoke because any coughing would tear at his stomach muscles. Anyway, the periods of dizziness were now almost continuous and he had to shake his head to retain any consciousness as he waited for the inevitable end, which he could no longer laugh off or keep at bay.

Regrets, of course he had regrets. No one wanted to die. If you were ninety-five you still didn't want to, the difference being if you can't go on living then how many of us can choose the time and place and the manner of their passing?

Looking around he decided that this was as good a place as any and his thoughts turned back home fleetingly, but he was unable to concentrate because of the waves of blankness that were sweeping across his consciousness. How long he lay there he would never know but he no longer had any feeling in his legs and his arms felt like lead.

He was brought to earth suddenly by the sound of voices, which came nearer and nearer. Suddenly and without further warning, they were there, about twenty of them. They hadn't seen him yet. Still they came on, closer and closer until, pointing his tommy gun in their general direction, he opened fire and saw four of them drop. The remainder took cover immediately and he continued to fire until his gun was empty. Changing to his last magazine he tried to pick them off one by one where he had seen them fall, until that too was empty.

Shaking himself, he took out his last grenade. *I'll wait until you show yourselves*, he thought. He removed the pin, tossed it to one side along with his empty gun, and lay back holding the primed grenade in his hand.

The enemy approached from both flanks, cautiously, with bayonets fixed, closing in quickly when they realised that he was out of ammo and seemingly defenceless. They drew back to lunge at him but he felt nothing. His muscles suddenly relaxed and his grip loosened on the grenade. Too late, before the Japs realised what was happening, there was a blinding flash, and before they could disengage their bayonets the spread of shrapnel cut down a further six.

The staccato bark of firing echoed across the valley, causing Tighe and his party to pause. The unmistakable sound of a grenade followed. Looking at each other there was no need to say anything. We all knew that any time gained now had been paid for in full.

There was no need to urge us on. We were now a good distance into the saddle pass and about to cut the main track. *Timing is now of the essence*, thought Tighe. The whole thrust of his strategy in shaking off our pursuers was to get the retreating Japs to do it for him. Tighe reckoned they were about half a day ahead of their pursuers, so he had sufficient time to position his men.

Leaving the Yank and Oz in a central position with a grandstand view of what he hoped would unfold, and high enough into the cliff to be out of harm's way, he placed himself together with me at one end of the ambush, and Douglas, Green and Taylor about 200 yards away at the far end. This would enable Yank and Oz to act as signallers between the two groups. Concealing themselves, they lay waiting in the baking afternoon sun, again losing unaffordable sweat.

It must have been some three hours later when we caught sight of the hand signal, higher up in the bluff, telling of the approach of our erstwhile pursuers. At the same time, the more noisy advance of the retreating Japanese forces appeared in the pass.

First to come into view was a mule driver with raised whip, repeatedly lashing and beating the unfortunate animal loaded down by the wheels of a mountain gun, one wheel strapped either side of its saddle. Alerting me, Tighe set his action on single shot. Taking careful aim, he shot the mule driver from about 120 yards. In the meantime I shot the mule, which collapsed without a sound, for in common with the animals that the British used they had their vocal chords cut to prevent them from braying and revealing their position.

The British drivers, however, treated their mules like royalty, giving them the best of their rations and whatever water was available. So attached were they to their charges that they invariably slept with them. The mules would follow them anywhere, such treatment being considered preferable to the whip.

Seeing the mule and driver dropped, the rest of the column topping the crest suddenly took cover. Douglas and Green heard the firing in the distance, prompting them to open fire on their former pursuers. Douglas found a target in one of the forward scouts and Green wounded the other one.

It was stalemate, until a grenade was lobbed down from above at each end, prompting a mortar response from both sides. The larger force put out scouts and called in a much heavier barrage, and by sheer weight of numbers, they overran their opponents.

What their thoughts must have been to discover that they had decimated their own, we could only conjecture.

Tighe's strategy had succeeded beyond his wildest dreams and we were finally rid of our pursuers. When things had calmed down and we felt it safe to move off we withdrew further into the bush, each of us aware of the fact that we would be able to get a good night's sleep without continually looking over our shoulders.

TWENTY-FIVE

WHEN THE LAST TWO GRENADES THROWN BY Howard and Cooke had decimated the Japanese flanking party, the spread of shrapnel had also killed more. Howard was already fatally wounded and Cooke had miraculously escaped any severe injury, except for a through and through wound in his left shoulder, but had been rendered unconscious by the explosion. The latter had probably saved his life, for when the enemy had advanced over their position they had considered him dead.

He came around just in time to see his comrades stand up and advance towards the enemy, and saw the last of them fall. He crawled over towards his mate, took his dog tag off and put him into some kind of military order, covering his face with his own hat. Then he made his way out by crawling through the cut perimeter fence to the edge of the jungle.

He couldn't check on the condition of any of his companions as the Nips were still wandering around. By this time, however, the limpet mines were exploding, and this finally made up his mind for him.

He considered his position. He was on his own, unarmed, with no compass, no food or water and nearly 200 miles from base camp. The only saving grace was that during daylight hours he would be able to see the saddle pass in the far distance and hopefully would be able to recognise some kind of track back to the rendezvous point.

He made himself an improvised sling for his left arm out of the right sleeve of his shirt. The wound looked clean enough; no bones broken, but it hurt like hell. However, he considered himself fortunate to have survived.

He cut himself a six-foot bamboo staff, sharpened it to a fine point, and set off at his best pace, trying to follow the way they had come.

The track he was following suddenly became more positive. Surely they hadn't cut this path? It suddenly dawned on him that he was following a

Japanese party when he came upon discarded cigarettes and food wrappers. What were they following? They were certainly being cautious.

The sound of mortar fire about four hours ahead coupled with the coming darkness encouraged him to cast around for somewhere to sleep for the night. The ground was out of the question. The only safe alternative was height, up a tree. He found one easy to climb, reckoning that forty feet was safe enough, and used his belt to secure himself in the cradle of a convenient raft of branches.

His shoulder was jumping like hell, as if he needed reminding. Inspecting it as best he could he decided that the missile, whatever it was, hadn't taken any fabric into the wound. Unfortunately any water he was able to risk damping wasn't clean enough to wash his shoulder, so he could only leave it alone and hope for the best.

Climbing down from his nest as dawn broke he continued to follow the well-defined track that was taking him steadily upwards.

Some four or five hours later, he was alerted by the smell of wood smoke, and he cautiously approached the outskirts of a small village. Lying up in dense cover, he observed the activity of the villagers and decided to risk entering. His stomach was growling for food and heavens only knew when he had last had a drink of water.

The village dogs came to meet him and escorted him, growling, to where the villagers were congregated. They seemed friendly enough, and invited him to eat and drink with them. He found out between bites that the Japanese had passed through and stayed only long enough to feed themselves and fill their water bottles, obviously in pursuit of his friends. He learnt that they had stayed with the villagers overnight and had disposed of the party of Japs that had been occupying them; they could only be two days ahead, although between them and himself were the pursuers.

After placing what food they could spare in his pack and filling his water bottle, the villagers showed Cooke where Tighe and his party had buried the Jap equipment. He selected a rifle and two hundred rounds of ammunition and wrapped the remainder up. As an afterthought, he packed six grenades that might come in handy. Thanking the headman, he strode with renewed hope and vigour back out onto the track. He was a lot less cautious until he nearly fell over the remains of a Nip soldier lying to one side. Obviously the victim of a grenade, he was in a number of pieces.

So Tighe had booby-trapped his retreat; normal procedure, but Cooke would have to be a lot more careful not to become a casualty himself. Forewarned is forearmed, so he cut a loop around the track for a couple of miles. A lot slower, but what the hell, better to arrive late than not.

Midday saw him standing on the edge of a clearing, where his mind was interpreting what his eyes were trying to tell him. This was obviously the result of the mortars that had fallen ahead of him yesterday, and his reading of the situation was confirmed. He was following a Japanese party, who in turn were following Tighe's section, who had extracted themselves from their target.

It was like walking into a slaughterhouse. At least two of the party had been killed. He recognised Bob Rogers and his mate, whose heads were still staring at each other. He couldn't leave them like this. At least the dog tags were missing, so someone else must have survived. After scraping a shallow hole in the bush with his bamboo stick, he placed the two heads side by side and covered them. The rest of the flesh lying about was too small to collect and had to be left behind.

Topping the rise, he decided to follow the dry watercourse. Judging by the disturbance of the river stones this was the obvious way they had gone. He was able to see quite a distance down the dry stream so he travelled at quite a pace.

Another day's travelling. After spending an uncomfortable night perched and tied up on a tree for safety, and still following the track, he came upon ten Jap bodies. What the hell had happened here? Finding and recognising Whitehouse, much mutilated, he began to piece things together in his mind.

Tighe wouldn't leave a single rearguard; Whitehouse must have been badly wounded, too badly to be carried. *Well done, old mate*, he thought. *You went to Valhalla well attended.* Taking the body to one side, he dug a shallow grave once more, and after taking Whitehouse's dog tag buried him as best he could.

This made three casualties. How many more burials would he have to preside over before this little lot was through? He didn't much care for his role of undertaker, but he couldn't allow his mates above ground to be violated by whatever crawled.

How far behind Tighe was he? More importantly, how far behind the pursuing Japs was he? He couldn't go bursting in on either of them or it might be the last move he made.

Looking far ahead he could see the An saddle pass looming up, so he decided to call it a day. Finding a likely tree, he went to bed in the security of the branches again, and despite being uncomfortable and surrounded by all the unnerving noises of the night he managed to get off to sleep.

A few more hours' travelling, the next day brought him into the beginnings of the pass, and he was cautiously aware it might become a thoroughfare. Climbing right into the bluff he was in time to see a mule and its driver being shot and the mini-action that followed. When everything had settled down he decided to risk trying to communicate with what he took to be the remnants of his own party.

Knowing a little Morse code, he took out his chromium-plated cigarette case. Using it as a mirror, he flashed SOS a number of times.

Tighe, who had caught the faint flashes, called me to read the message.

"SOS, Sarge." Then I replied, "Who?"

The garbled answer came back.

"Hope he can read better than he can send," I murmured, and flashed slowly, "Come in."

Making what he thought was 'R', Cooke noted the spot where the light had replied from and made his way with difficulty to the spot. He found no one there.

Suddenly he was surrounded by armed men. "I'm on my own, Sarge," he said. "No one else will be coming back, but the job was done. Everything was destroyed; mission successful." He went on to describe the action and the trek to join us; how he had buried Rogers' remains, his mate and Whitehouse's; how Whitehouse had taken ten with him. Cooke gave Whitehouse's dog tag to Tighe.

"Do you feel fit to go on, Cooke?"

"Sure, Sarge, just say the word. Glad to be with company again. I called in at the village after you and the Japs had passed through in too much of a hurry to catch you up to do any damage, although your grenade accounted for one of them on the track."

"Thanks for the report; sorry about the rest of your team. I'm glad you made it. Let's have a look at your shoulder."

"Its not too bad, Sarge. A bit stiff, but I haven't been able to clean it."

"Looks as if it's healing well. Looks healthy enough. I think I've got a bit of sulphur powder left." Tighe sprinkled it over the wound and bound it up with a strip from his own shirt. Cooke went to join the rest of the party, who were scraping a few rations together.

TWENTY-SIX

TIGHE WAS FULLY AWARE THAT WHATEVER PLAN he had formulated was only valid until it was put into practice, and from then on it would have to be played off the cuff.

The next objective was to reach the ferry over the Lemro River, and to hope that it was working. If it wasn't we were in all kinds of trouble. The Lemro itself, next to the Irrawaddi, was one of the major rivers on the Arakan Peninsula and it had to be crossed.

Returning to base by the more northerly route to avoid the retreating Japanese would necessarily take us through the flood plains. Tighe's much-viewed map detailed metalled roads and jeepable tracks. The metalled roads we would have to avoid, likewise the jeepable tracks, which all took the same route close to the banks of the river and were likely to be busy with questionable traffic.

After discussing the options, we decided to head for the ferry, which was situated between the villages of Panmyaung and Minbar, separated by about twelve miles. Any casual traffic that probably used it by day would have to be avoided, so we had to prepare for a night crossing. It would be possible to pinpoint our objective with reasonable accuracy if we could pass close to the settlements of Butalon, Shwelan and Myaungbwe. The passage, however, would be a tortuous one, passing through rubber plantations, rice paddy fields and mangrove swamps. The first two problems would have to be skirted around to avoid the local population and the swamps avoided altogether because of the alligator inhabitants.

What additional mileage this would entail we could only imagine, but to go through these settlements not knowing whether the inhabitants were friendly or not was not worth the risk. The little settlement that we had already liberated from the rogue Japanese section had proved friendly enough, but was that just

138

their relief at being freed from their occupation? All these scattered settlements might not be so friendly and we couldn't take the chance.

We debated long into the night whether to ditch the two LMGs (light machine guns) and their ten belts of ammunition that we had accumulated courtesy of our last encounter with the enemy. Was it worth the extra carry? After careful consideration we decided to continue to shoulder them but to rotate more frequently. We also decided to bring along a good supply of Japanese grenades to supplement our own.

After lying up overnight, we pushed on through the next morning. No breakfast, no water; both had long since gone. Tighe took the precaution of putting out a forward scout. No flankers; he hadn't enough men, so we had to rely on our instincts and bushcraft.

Visibility as usual was severely curtailed, the encroaching jungle pressing in on us from all sides, but it was the thinning of the vegetation that presented the biggest worry. Where there were clearings you always found plantations, and that meant people, something we were trying to avoid. Human activity was obvious; the trunks of the rubber trees bore recent evidence of circular bark-cutting just above the cups suspended to catch the latex. This meant going to ground until the area had been declared safe to cross. Tedious but necessary. All this yomping was done in complete silence until the forward scout held up his hand and we closed up on him to find that he had discovered a tamarind tree at the side of the track.

The prospect of food soon had us all collecting the long pods, like broad beans, hanging in profusion on the branches. Like a swarm of locusts, we collected all the ones that had fallen to the ground as well. These pods were crammed with sweet nutritious food. The hard, black, indigestible seed we had to spit out. This bounty would be sufficient to last us for some days, used judiciously.

We came across the odd plantain palm, but the banana-like fruit was totally inedible and as hard as your mother-in-law's heart, so we pushed on.

The Myaungbwe *chaung*, a tributary that the map showed feeding into the Lemro, would be our preferred way to travel, but we had no boat. We couldn't find one so we had to continue slogging. The map also showed that the tributary was served by a small ferry connecting it to the metalled road; unfortunately we had to avoid both.

As we approached Myaungbwe itself, we could see a pagoda, a mosque, and rows of graves. Civilisation. We didn't need it! So we took a bearing north, towards the little settlement of Kyindwa, that would take us across the metalled road, which sported a telegraph line. Should we cut it, or would that only betray our presence? We decided to leave it intact, reasoning that it would draw attention to the ferry itself.

As we approached the ferry point we lay up to check the activity. It appeared to be used by native traffic only; bullock carts, handcarts, and the occasional foot passenger. We couldn't use the crossing by day as we would stand out like the proverbial sore thumb, so we waited for darkness. We discussed our options. There was an office. Was there a ferry master? Must be. Night shift? Did the crews go home? Did any sleep on site? We would have to wait to find out.

There appeared to be two boats. The big one was wood-burning and the smaller one was operated by hauling on a rope, something we could do ourselves.

Whilst waiting for darkness we saw the stack on the wood burner being shut down and the operators making their way towards the main settlement. Cookie and I were detailed to suss out the position at the jetty, and we reported it all clear, no guards.

Making our way to the hand-operated ferry we went on board and stowed our gear along the thwarts. When casting off, we all needed to pull on the rope that was to take us to the other side, some one hundred and fifty yards against a tidal current that was fast ebbing to the sea.

With the occasional pause from our unnatural exertions, we finally made it to the other side. We unloaded and found natural ground cover automatically. Even if it wasn't necessary we did so habitually for safety. The only problem now was the ferryboat. It was on the wrong side of the river, so we decided to pull it back to the other side. We couldn't tie it up, but what the hell. One of the operating crew would probably carry the can.

Toting our gear again, we headed off by moonlight towards Minbu, where we hoped to lie up for the rest of the night.

Minbu was quite an extensive village area, if the map was anything to go by; some fifty or sixty huts, some occupied, the rest either deserted or destroyed. The next day saw us across the Panmaungyi *chaung*. These *chaungs* were as numerous as country lanes back home and were used by the locals as communication highways. A small boat took the place of a car, and they could be seen paddling along in the middle of nowhere, without a care in the world.

We were now approaching the forest area again and we struck out for Paledung, from where we could set a course for Myebon, and from there Akyab, which was our last port of call before we could consider ourselves home and dry.

The track became much steeper as we approached Myebon, and we had to make use of our entrenching tool picks to gain any height at all. Suddenly, without any warning, the forward scout, Davies, held up his hand, our prearranged signal for danger, and we dropped flat.

"I think we've been spotted, Sarge," he said. "A party of Japs coming this way. About twenty-five. I'm pretty sure they've started to deploy!"

"Right, shift your arses!" yelled Tighe. "We need height. We can't defend this area. Move up as quick as you can to the crest of the rise and dig in. Make like moles, arrowhead formation. Lambert, you take the point. The rest of you fan out above to give yourselves a clear field of fire."

Fortunately, it was beginning to get dark, so the activity of digging was not obvious. Shallow scrapes were no good – no protection. The entrenching tools were quite efficient, and the earth they threw up on the down slope would double the cover, at least from small arms fire.

The Japs wouldn't attack in the half light; they would wait for darkness and try the covert approach. The two LMGs had been set up on the flanks, and the Marines had laid the captured grenades to hand.

"Let them come to us, lads," said Tighe. "Don't be trigger-happy. Wait until I put the flare up, and then only on single shot unless they advance in a bunch, which they won't if they have any sense."

Seven of us, thought Tighe, *plus the Oz and the Yank, against about twenty. Not bad odds, and at least it's in a position of our own choosing.*

Tighe had set up the defensive position in an arrowhead formation. The forward position was occupied by me – I having drawn the short straw. Two positions set further up the slope – thirty feet away – were occupied by Taylor and Douglas, and the final four were some forty feet away where Jones and Green were hunkered down. Yank and Oz shared the centre position, which

141

Tighe had helped them to dig to give them the maximum protection. Tighe himself would be a floater, strengthening the position under the heaviest attack.

I lay sideways in my trench, not daring to move. My eyes, accustomed to the dark, could pick out a shape crawling towards my position. The hair on the back of my neck began to rise and sweat started to trickle down my face. The most ancient of all atavistic fears, deeply embedded in the primeval brain of the reptile, and still active countless millennia after we had left the fastness of the sea and caverns, warned me that something was moving out there. I had to let my attacker come to me. Silhouetted vaguely against the lighter horizon, he was making his move. The only weapon he appeared to have was a knife, which was clenched between his teeth. He obviously recognised by touch the excavated earth that I had thrown forward, and he paused momentarily, trying to figure out exactly where I was.

Waiting for him to make his move was the worst time. I couldn't go to meet him and lose the advantage. I still had to wait.

Suddenly making up his mind, he stood up and threw himself over the parapet, fully expecting to land on me, but I wasn't there. I came at him from the side and fell across him where he had landed. My own knife took him in the throat in an upward motion, driving it through to the base of his skull.

He choked and gurgled as he sprayed blood from his mouth and splattered my face. *Inconsiderate bastard*, I thought. *Still, better his blood than mine.* His eyes rounded in terror as he fought against his own death. A choking stench rose up, as first his bladder then his bowels voided in a foetid gush, then his spasms quieted as he finally let go and I dumped him on the parapet to provide a little more protection.

Although it had all happened in relative silence, the sound of the scuffling must have carried to Tighe, which was enough for him to put the first flare up. It hung on its parachute and illuminated the whole of the hillside, etching the attackers in great detail. The grenades were the first weapons the defenders unleashed and they exploded amongst the crawling men. Another flare followed the first, showing the enemy scrambling back down the hill. These proved easy targets and we double tapped them with our stens. The machine guns from the flanks joined in the carnage, finishing off those wounded who had managed to crawl away.

The silence was unreal as we waited for any retaliation. There was none. We went forward and carefully checked each corpse. Only two were playing possum, and they too went to join their honourable ancestors. Any food or water that that was found in their packs was confiscated before we decided to hotfoot it out of the area.

It was decided to leave one of the machine guns and a couple of grenades to cause confusion and pose any investigation with the question of "Who killed the little sons of heaven with their own guns?" That should cloud or minimise any pursuit.

"No injuries anyone?" said Tighe. "Let's move before we have visitors."

Caution still dictated that we should travel in the foothills, skirting Myebon and Myohaung, and head for Paletwa before turning towards the coast to finally head for Cox`s Bazaar, which we were sure was still in British hands.

With the arduous nature of the An Pass behind us and the flood plains safely negotiated, the prospect of a safe emergence from the jungle could be anticipated but not taken for granted. Caution still had to be uppermost in all our minds; it would be stupid to throw it all away due to a moment's carelessness.

A pre-monsoon storm that had lashed the area the previous night made the footings precarious, and the early morning sun lanced through the jungle canopy and illuminated the myriad spiders' webs catching the raindrops and dew that clung to them, transforming them into diadems and strings of pearls.

The ever-present sun, however, would reach its zenith and rule over everything with a sullen ferocity, but the overnight flash storm, the herald of the approaching monsoon season, at least gave us a plentiful supply of fresh water, which we collected, strained through our shirts and dosed with water purifying tablets, before topping up our bottles.

The main concern for our own comfort was food. The finding of the tamarind tree had been a godsend, but that had long since been exhausted. Living off the land is fine in principle, so long as there is something edible about. There is no doubt that there was plenty to eat if you were willing to experiment, but going hungry for a few days more wouldn't hurt and we could put up with it so long as we had prospects. It was merely a question of tightening our belts up a couple of notches and ignoring the growling stomachs.

Twenty-seven

S TILL FIXED IN OUR MINDS WAS THE thought of the remnants of the Indian troops who had joined the Japanese at the height of their offensive, whose whereabouts were still unknown, and who wouldn't be friendly, and who could still prove to be a threat to our safe emergence from the jungle, unless they decided to change sides again.

We had no fear of pursuit from the rear. The retreating enemy had already disposed of that threat, but any signs of habitation, betrayed by either wood smoke or well-trodden tracks, would have to be detoured with special care. Even the smells of cooking seemed to beckon us with a persistence almost irresistible.

Nuts and berries collected along the way now formed the main part of our diet. To find a nest of eggs, however dubious, was a special treat and they were pierced and sucked with great relish.

I brought a wild piglet down with a bow-shot, and however tempting it appeared we resisted the urge to rush and collect it in case its last squeal alerted a vengeful sow or boar. The latter was to be avoided at all costs. Nothing short of death would deter an irate single-minded individual armed with death-dealing tusks.

We withdrew into the sheltering lea of an overhanging shelf of rock, allowing enough time to elapse to consider it safe to recover the piglet. When we considered it safe, we cleaned it, cut it up and spitted it over a smokeless bamboo fire. The smells that emanated around the makeshift roasting were almost a meal in themselves. As it was young pork it was decided to cook it in strips, and overcook it to make sure that it was thoroughly done. The outer skin was burned black, but that did not detract from a most agreeable meal, the first substantial one in over a week.

After finding a small rock-pool, we cleared the detritus from the surface and strained it through someone's clean shirt, then waited for a sterilizing tablet to do its work before washing away the traces of burnt crackling from our mouths.

Towards dusk, we concealed ourselves in a stand of bamboo to get some sleep. Being lodged in bamboo was as good as being fenced in, and we always chose these sites as being the most secure. Spirits were raised somewhat as we hoped that this would be our last night before emerging from the jungle, if Tighe's compass and calculations were correct.

Looking around he took stock of his little band. Douglas, Taylor, Green, Lambert, Jones, Cooke and himself. *Just seven of us left out of a force of twenty*, he thought, *plus the two ex-prisoners, Yank and Oz.*

He decided to stand the watch himself to give everyone a chance to recharge their batteries. What they had achieved during the past eighteen days against all that the enemy could throw at them was nothing short of miraculous.

They had achieved their objective, but at what a cost. They all knew at the outset that it was probably suicidal, but none of them had hesitated. They had all wanted to be a part of it, believing that in the overall scheme of things it was worthwhile. Anyway, the belief always is that it is the next man who will be a casualty, never yourself.

Tighe's train of thought was broken by Daisy Green, who came to relieve him and to take the morning watch. They exchanged only cursory remarks before Tighe moved away to find a suitable bed space. However, a quiet mind is a prerequisite for sleep, and whether it was due to responsibility, weight of command, or the overriding desire and determination to survive, sleep evaded him almost until dawn.

We had now decided to travel during the day and we pushed on towards the towering Blue Mountains that reared up some 7,000 feet in the far distance. Skirting what we took to be Paletwa we struck out at right angles for the coast, hoping we had gone far enough north to emerge in the direction of Cox's Bazaar.

The jungle had now begun to thin out, to be replaced by broken shrub. Suddenly we emerged onto a dirt road, and Tighe stationed us in single file either side of the road with weapons at the ready. No one was ready to take any chances; everyone was to be considered hostile until proved otherwise.

After about ten miles we began to pass through cultivated fields. We recognized a type of corn, hoed-up rows of pineapples and lagoon-like paddy fields. Scattered locals at work straightened up as we passed and put up their hands, shielding their eyes to view the motley collection of scarecrows, all in a strange silence. Then they bent down again and got on with their tasks as if nothing had happened.

Thinking about it, they had seen it all before, the only difference was the colour of the skin and the uniform. It had happened over countless centuries before. Conquerors, occupiers made no difference to them; the only things that remained unchanged were the native peoples themselves.

Native women walked towards us, obviously on their way to Paletwa, large wicker baskets loaded with aluminium pots and cooking utensils on their heads. They passed in silence, neither group being able to understand the other.

Passing along the only way through a village, with shops on either side, we eyed with watering mouths the piles of fruit and vegetables offered for sale. Having no money, however, we were viewed with suspicion, although if we had been able to make our plight known the villagers would probably have helped us. The only thing that was free was the water, and we filled up our bottles and drank what we could before moving on.

Some little distance further on the dirt road gave way to a patched and tarmac-covered road. Calling a halt and assembling us into closed-up files, Tighe said in his parade ground voice, "Straighten yourselves up, sling your arms and march like Marines. I don't care what the hell you look like, but at least you'll act like Marines."

The road sign said in Indian and English, 'COX'S BAZAAR nine miles'.

"What a marvellous bloody sight. Never thought we would make it," said Daisy Green to no one in particular.

"Neither did I," returned Douglas, "but I'd like to see anyone stop us now."

Left, Right, Left, Right. *Has it all been worth it?* thought Tighe. All those beautiful young men on the threshold of life – cut down in their prime.

No time to ponder that now. Our interest was drawn to the sides of the road. Spaced at regular intervals and seated on their woven mats were the eternal beggars, shaking their cups, imploring alms. So grotesque were the attitudes of some of their limbs that it was suggested that their parents had deliberately deformed them at birth to enable them to ply the trade of begging. Their relatives brought both them and their mats to the side of the road to solicit alms.

Whilst passing a bend in the road that obviously followed the course of a wide river we paused to watch a group of dhobi wallahs beating the hell out of clothes against large flat rocks that lined the banks of the river. Surrounding everything were the huge rafts of saris that had been washed and spread on the low scrub to dry, their bright colours rippling like multicoloured flags in the hot midday sun.

Stepping out of line to allow the last two in the column to catch up with him, Tighe spoke to the Yank and Oz. They were holding up quite well but were obviously in worse shape than the Marines.

"I'm planning to pick up the main road or to find some kind of coastal transport up to Chittagong or down the coast to Akyab. You can either drop off at Cox's Bazaar and make your own arrangements—"

Before he could finish and without looking at each other they both said in unison, "We'll stay, Sarge, as long as we can. We don't think you could manage without us."

With just the trace of a smile, Tighe intimated that he would be glad of their company and left to take his place at the front of the little band. The flow of traffic was beginning to increase now as we made our way through the outskirts of the village and finally out onto the main road. The locals made way for us to pass, possibly because we looked so disreputable.

The seventy-five miles to Chittagong were daunting, but the problem of finding some form of transport without the money to pay for it was solved for us by an RN truck pulling up ahead.

A lieutenant climbed down from the cab and with some amazement offered us a ride. We climbed in the back and sat amongst the stores that littered the floor of the truck. After easing off our packs, we lay back against the sides of the canvas-clad vehicle, thankful to take the weight off our feet at last.

Tighe, who sat between the driver and the officer, accepted a tin of cigarettes, took one for himself, and passed the tin back to his men. Together we enjoyed our first smoke for many days.

The miles passed. Tighe arranged with the officer to drop us off about half a mile from the naval base, except for the two ex-prisoners, who would be driven straight to the sickbay in the camp where they would receive proper medical care.

At the dropping-off point it was, "Fall in, in single file, straighten your clothes, sling your arms, and march." Feet that had walked more than 200 miles over some of the worst terrain in the world, and that had received no tender loving care, took a lot of motivating, particularly as they had been rested for so long. Blisters had burst and every contour of the uneven surface awakened spasms of pain, but the thought that the end was in sight kept us going.

Again the thought returned to Tighe, had it all been worth it? In ten years' time who would remember except those who had survived? Their achievements would be forgotten or buried on one page of some biographer's memoirs. Lost forever would be the record and recognition of the uncommon valour that had been the common currency of this band of men.

He could only conjecture at what the talk shops that would probably be set up at the end of the war would do with a peace that had been wrested at such a cost from the evil that had virtually encompassed the whole world.

What the politicians had done, or had failed to do, with the peace between the wars was nothing short of criminal. The League of Nations set up by the victorious countries had turned out to be a waste of time. No direction. No teeth. No cohesion. Perhaps the major powers needed to cooperate, despite their various ideologies, and take in tow the smaller nations, subscribing to some kind of rapid reaction force to act decisively and quickly to deter any would-be aggressor.

To stand by wringing hands and allow an oppressive regime to establish itself, either through coercion by its rulers or complacency by its neighbours, would be nothing short of criminal. Human nature being what it was, though, some country would always look enviously at its neighbour's possessions and endeavour to redraw its boundaries.

It appeared to Tighe that the poorest countries would always strive to find monies to possess the greatest quantities of arms, perhaps to satisfy some nationalistic ego, or to give weight to their voice in any international deliberations.

The further he travelled the more he reckoned that religion had much to answer for, since the days of the Inquisition and the religious persecutions and excesses of the Dark Ages, all in the name of their people's own deity, and in some cases, sadly, the same deity.

The poorer the country the finer and more lavish the places of worship appeared to be. A cynical point of view, perhaps, was that they were being used as an opiate to ensure the people's servility. It says a lot for religious teachings that the only one of God's instructions that was practised with any fervour was to go forth and multiply.

Even the Victorians propagated and instilled in the very young a message of compliance, with hymns saying God made them high or lowly and ordered their estate. Nothing bright and beautiful about that.

Those unfortunate enough not to survive should have a legacy – the turning of their hopes and aspirations of a better tomorrow into reality. And when the peace bells finally rang out and the big boys back at home had congratulated themselves and mutually ennobled themselves with their stars and medals, it was to be hoped that they would sometimes remember the scattered crosses that littered the seven continents. To mark the sacrifices that enabled them to survive, perhaps the great and the good would do more than just stand on their chalk-marked places in front of the local cenotaphs once a year, walking away satisfied and feeling good for being seen doing what was expected.

The war should not be allowed to vanish into the obscurity of future ages. The careless onrushing winds of time would bury such achievements deep within history's cynical dust, and no amount of archaeology would or could uncover it.

The politically correct brigades could and probably would attempt to sweep these atrocities under the carpet for fear of hurting people's finer feelings, and by doing so create the appalling prospect that it could happen again.

Children probably wouldn't be taught about it at school, fostering a legacy that would hold it never happened, or was too appalling to have happened. In the countries in whose names these atrocities were perpetrated they would be denied, being too enormous to contemplate.

The gated entrance of the Royal Naval Establishment came into view and the two sentries came sharply to attention and gave the little party a 'Butt' salute.

The naval lieutenant, who had suspected that he had been privileged to witness the end of something special, had alerted the guard commander. The guard had been fallen in and were standing stiffly to attention, uniforms in pussers (first class) military condition, with white blancoed belts and gaiters. Rifles went from the 'slope' to the 'present' in precise military timing.

Tighe returned the salute as we marched through the gates into the camp, to be received and absorbed once again into the brotherhood that had nurtured us.

TWENTY-EIGHT

A S WE ENTERED THE CONFINES OF THE camp we were greeted by the commandant and surrounded by groups of curious officers, all wanting to know the whos, whys and wherefores. The CO, however, escorted us to the mess hall, where the cooks fell over themselves to lay on the kind of food we hadn't seen for a month.

"From here, when you have finished in the mess hall, Sergeant Tighe, I want you over at the sickbay, and from there to the showers, and then bed rest. Then I shall be looking forward to your account in detail."

It took a week for all the preliminaries to be put to bed, and with showers, new issue of kit and regular rest we were almost back to normal and fitting in with life on the base. We were still viewed with interest, however, and with Tighe being called to the Company Office we were looking forward to having our speculations settled.

"Sit down, Sergeant. Make yourself comfortable. Cigarette? Drink? Start at the beginning. We want to hear a preliminary report; you can fill in the details later. I'm Lieutenant-Colonel John Maltravers, and this is my adjutant, Captain Charles Perry. Please carry on in your own time, we've already spoken briefly to the Yank and the Oz, as you call them. They are in sickbay, so we are in possession of some of the facts. They are progressing quite well, and frankly from the little they were able to tell us we were expecting you and your men to be at least ten feet tall!"

Starting from when the attack went in, Tighe took them through the whole report in sequence, detailing the parts that all of us had played, and the assumed loss of Captain Newsome and his party that was later confirmed by Marine Cooke when he rejoined them. Glossing over his own contribution, he described the rescue of the prisoners, the destruction of the oilfields, and the sacrifices of some of his men. "I cannot speak too highly of my men, sir. They have done all that was asked of them and more, and any thanks that may be due is solely theirs. Without them, the job couldn't have been done and they have more than upheld the honour of the Corps. I have been proud and privileged to be associated with them."

"Thank you, Sergeant, a most concise and revealing report. I shall have to ask you to put it into writing at some point. In the meantime, we should like to shake your hand, the Captain and myself, and say what a great honour it is to know both yourself and your men. What you have achieved is remarkable and reflects honour, both on yourselves and the Corps in the very highest traditions. Frankly, we expected nothing less. Thank you again, Sergeant. I shall make arrangements for both yourself and your men to enjoy a week's local leave to help you unwind, and when you come back we shall have to consider your placement."

"Together with my men would be a privilege, sir."

"We'll see what can be done."

"Thank you, sir." Tighe saluted and left the office.

When he had left, the CO said, "Charles, we cannot let this go unnoticed. This achievement is too great for that. I intend to have a word with the top brass and see what should be done. I most certainly recommend an award of some sort. Get me SEAC on the air and we'll push it that far up, to Lord Louis if necessary."

After getting his men together Tighe gave us the good news about the week's local leave, and we looked forward to the freedom that it promised. "Before we can go, lads, I have to go back to the Company Office. Something I forgot to do."

"Sergeant Tighe to see the CO," the orderly announced.

"Come in, Sergeant. What can I do for you?"

"Unforgivable of me, sir. I have a number of dog tags in my possession, and I would like to ask your permission for me to write to their next of kin. It is something I feel I must do to put some kind of closure on all that has happened. I feel I owe it to them all."

"Certainly, Sergeant, by all means. I can think of no better person to do it, and I should deem it a privilege to add a few words myself."

Tighe spent the next couple of days composing letters to the next of kin. He then passed them over to the company office for closure and forwarding.

A week's leave isn't long, despite all the new sights and experiences, yet it can be too long when you've got nothing to do, only pleasing yourself. It came to an end, thankfully, like all things do, and we settled into a more regimented routine; not square-bashing, just lectures and tactics. Then, out of the blue, Tighe was summoned by the CO.

"Sit down, Sergeant," the CO said. Without further preamble he added, "I am pleased to inform you that you have been awarded a field commission. You are now officially Second Lieutenant. J.T. Tighe, an officer and a gentleman, by act of Parliament and His Majesty the King. Congratulations, and well-deserved. You have also been awarded the DSO, and it will be presented to you at a ceremony at Cochin by Mountbatten himself. How do you feel, Lieutanant?"

"Too much to take in, sir, but the credit must go to my men. Without them it couldn't have happened."

"They haven't been overlooked. Corporal Winters has been upgraded to Sergeant, with a mention. Jones, Green, Douglas and Lambert have all been given a stripe, and a mention. Also, Marine Cooke from Captain Newsome's team has been mentioned in despatches, together with the men you left behind. It may be some small comfort to those back at home. Arrangements are being made to fly you all to Cochin to receive your awards, and two weeks' leave. In the meantime, welcome to the wardroom, Lieutenant. You will all draw your new uniforms for the presentation, and whatever kit you require. You've got about three days to prepare yourselves and, Lieutenant, I'd be honoured if you would accept two of my pips."

"Thank you, sir."

Standing on the veranda outside the office, Tighe tried to clear his head. It was too much to digest, too much. He'd better tell his men and get ready for the salutes and handshake.

The flight to Cochin in India was in an old Dakota, the workhorse of the RAF, and after a three-hour flight we landed and were transported to the nearest naval base.

The procedure and protocol to be followed at the ceremony were explained and, come the day, the parade ground seemed huge. Long lines of service personnel were assembled, army, navy and air force; the recipients of awards were lined up, and the White Knight arrived in a jeep, dressed in full crisp and white naval uniform – number ones.

Tighe and the rest of us had been assembled to one side as though an afterthought. Standing rigidly to attention we waited the arrival of Lord Louis Mountbatten, who paused as his aide said, "Lieutenant Tighe, Royal Marines, DSO."

"Lieutenant Tighe, I have read your report and I am delighted and over-whelmed at what you and your men have achieved. Your awards are fully justified. Congratulations."

Tighe saluted and stepped back. *Thank God that's all over*, he thought. *Now let's get back to reality and normality.*

Normality meant packing kit and preparing for transportation to the Hill Station in the Nilgiri Hills, for two weeks leave in Ootacamund. This area was green and pleasant, much cooler than the plains, and you were able to sleep, still under mosquito netting, but much more comfortable.

The shops and cafés that lined the main street were a delight and happy hours were spent sampling what was on offer. Not being able to share the same billet as his men, Tighe was at last forced to accept his changed status, but his former companions took it all in their stride, and as all servicemen will confirm, you salute the uniform, not the man. Anything else, coupled with respect, had to be earned, and we considered he had.

We flew back to Chittagong after our short break and joined our new squads, settling in as part of a new family, taking up the required chores and practices. We were still viewed with some kind of awe and a lot was expected of us, as we were amongst untrained men, recently out from England and still acclimatising.

Twenty-nine

THE DISCUSSIONS THAT TOOK PLACE IN THE officers' mess were intended to bring Lt. Tighe up-to-date and fill in the blanks about events that had taken place during the past few weeks.

He already knew about the loss of the two British capital ships, the *Prince of Wales* and the *Repulse*, also the requested Hurricane fighter protection that never materialised. The consensus of opinion was that no lessons had been learned in spite of the naval action a year earlier when twenty British aircraft had flown from a carrier in the Mediterranean to attack the Italian battle fleet in Taranto harbour, sinking three battleships at their moorings. The Japs could possibly have used that engagement as a blueprint for the attack on Pearl Harbour.

The officers tried to put the progress of the war into some kind of perspective, tracing events from the German declaration of war on America, from her being neutral in Europe. Now she would have to fight on two fronts. Naturally, America would be preoccupied with the war against Japan, and the Atlantic lifeline would still be in the care of the British and Canadian navies, who would still have to shuttle to and fro with vital war materials.

The German U-boats were still a menace, and to counter this American Liberty Ships, better known as Woolworths Navy, so unstable that they reputedly could roll on wet grass, complemented the make-do aircraft carriers.

No one liked the way that the South of Ireland had declared her neutrality, although she herself interpreted this with typical Irish flair, permitting the Germans to set up and maintain an espionage centre in Dublin. This back door into Britain, that was to be kept open during the whole of the war, did immeasurable damage to the Allied cause.

"How about the loss of the naval bases in the South of Ireland that were available during the First World War?" one Rupert (junior officer) asked.

"Doesn't matter," came the quick reply. "She is perfectly within her strict legal rights to stand aside from the Allied fight."

"That doesn't make it less of a tongue-in-cheek neutrality though, and no amount of Blarney Stone rhetoric and flashing Irish eyes will eliminate the tally of Allied lives and ships that may be attributable to this policy."

The cut and thrust of the discussion became quite heated. "Think of her neutrality, though. Her neutrality is virtually guaranteed by her close proximity to Britain, and if Jerry were to start putting troops and equipment in there we should be within our strict legal rights too to bomb the hell out of her."

"She has a lot of support across in the States, though. Just imagine the Irish American bars crowded with first, second and third generation Irish Americans singing nostalgically into their beers about 'taking Kathleen home again'. They may well be advised to ask Kathleen if she wanted to go back again. She could be too ashamed to do so."

"Shouldn't this have been her fight too? For the chances of self-expression and freedom in the event of a German victory are virtually non-existent. She would suffer, together with Britain, under the Teutonic yoke."

"Don't think that everyone loves us Brits. Perhaps it was perceived in some quarters that as a result of this neutrality, and in the event of Britain's defeat, she would gain that which her bombs and bullets couldn't. I understand that the army council of the IRA who were reputed to have visited Nazi Germany may have seen Britain's discomfort as a window of opportunity."

"I don't think that any of us should forget that, however it may be viewed in retrospect, to their great credit large number of citizens of this country of their own accord came across the water to join many of our armed services and are serving with great distinction. In fact, our services are much the better for their participation, and a lot of our successes are due in a large part to their support."

"Ah well," Tighe murmured, "this has been a most interesting evening. Thanks for the company, the history lesson and the free-flowing bar, but I'm for my charpoy. Got a long day tomorrow. Goodnight all."

THIRTY

THE BEGINNING OF THE MONSOON SEASON BROUGHT blessed relief. The lowering black clouds seemed to empty their contents for days on end with scarcely a break. After suffering sticky nights tossing and turning on our charpoys the continuous rain hammering down on the corrugated iron roofs was preferable to the insufferable heat.

Another bonus was that the temperature and rain brought temporary relief from the perpetual droning of the mosquitoes. When they stopped droning they had landed on you and were using you as an all-night café. The rows of angry spots would indicate where they had dined during the night.

It was too wet for drill or any other activity on the square. The powers that be were at a loss over how to fill the day; perhaps the odd lecture or a night-time game of housey-housey. There was the odd visit to the *basha* that was used as a canteen to collect your weekly ration of two bottles of beer. Otherwise the eternal card schools were some kind of relief from the boredom.

Some planner slipped up when they didn't cater for a drill shed, or for somewhere under cover where the men could whitewash stones ready to be set around the officers' quarters and the camp perimeter.

Meanwhile in the officers' mess Tighe continued to be made very welcome, especially by the CO and his adjutant, but the fact that he had come up from the ranks, not the recognised route of University and OCTU, made him feel more than a little uncomfortable.

Under normal circumstances, he might have felt inferior, but his length of service as a regular and ten years' experience helped him to put these white-kneed HO Ruperts into perspective. Not that they were anything but polite, but things took on a more friendly atmosphere when he put up his DSO ribbon. Then he suddenly became popular, and flavour of the month.

157

The days of sun, wine and roses had to come to an end, and they did when a flotilla of landing craft were delivered and we were sorted out into crews. These mechanised landing craft could be, and often were, used as workhorses, delivering stores and supplies.

The landing at Ruywa by the Indian army required the transport of a large quantity of mules to be used to carry the mountain artillery and heavy stores. The sight of these creatures braying to the heavens without making a sound was disturbing, and we realised that their vocal chords had been cut for the same reason as the Japanese mules.

Tighe and his crew also picked up and transported three companies of West African Troops. These fearsome-looking soldiers with deeply cut tribal marks on their faces were frightening enough without weapons; they were fiercely loyal to their English officers and would follow them to hell and back. They were more at home in the jungle than even their Japanese enemies, and together with the Gurkhas were the most feared by them.

They went silently, barefoot, and would despatch their enemies before they knew they were amongst them, using their inborn bushcraft and natural weapons, the knife and *panga*, although they were fully armed with rifle and revolver.

Rangoon had now fallen to the Allied assault and Tighe and his crew were detailed to repatriate a schoolteacher and her family, who had been held captive during the Japanese occupation, to their home on Cheduba Island. This was a round trip of some three days, and upon landing, they were invited to the island's schoolhouse where they were to sleep over.

Tying up their LCM 454 craft, they were to be discovered by a Japanese gunboat that opened fire and sunk them. With no means of communication, they had to wait for about a week until they were considered overdue and for a relief craft to come and find them. In the meantime, they were made welcome in the village and were aided by the schoolteacher who had been educated in Rangoon and was fluent in English.

Back at base, they were loaded onto LST 406, a tank-landing ship, to be transported to Malaya and Singapore and to lie up close to the Johore Straits to be readied for the retaking of these possessions, so meekly surrendered on the 14th February 1942.

This had been possibly the most comprehensive defeat in the history of the British Army in World War II. The speed and brutality of the Japanese army clearly illustrated how they were to fight in the Far Eastern theatre of war, and could be seen as a continuation of the atrocities perpetrated in Nanking, China.

British troops stationed in Singapore were told by their officers that the Japanese were poor fighters, but the speed and ferocity of their advance down the Malayan Peninsula took everyone by surprise. This was the first time that the British had come under a full-scale enemy attack.

Any ideas that were harboured of the Japanese fighting a conventional war were soon dismissed. Expecting a frontal attack from the sea they were totally unprepared. It was not conceived by the British military top brass that the Japs could attack in any other way, especially through the difficult mangrove swamps and jungle. They were confounded that this was precisely the route they took. Sitting in their air-conditioned luxury and sipping Singapore Slings in Raffles Hotel, the British waited for something they were confident would never arise, secure behind their defences and big guns.

The Japanese attacked down the Peninsula and were told to take no prisoners, as they would slow down their advance. When a Japanese contingent landed at Kota Bharu airport, in Malaya, such was the complacency of the British Governor, Sir Shenton Thomas, he is alleged to have said to the army chiefs, "I suppose you will have to go push the little men off, then."

Almost all the RAF planes had been destroyed when the Japanese attacked the airfields in Singapore, so the army would receive no air support. It was left to the army to stem the advance, led by Lt. General Sir Arthur Percival. His force, numbering perhaps 90,000 to 100,000 men, comprised British, Australian and Indian troops, many of whom were green, untested and hadn't fired a shot in anger. They were opposed by 65,000 Japanese troops, battle hardened in the Chinese campaign, led by General Tomoyuki Yamashita.

Percival and his troops, were soundly beaten at the Battle of Jitra in early December and were subsequently in full retreat. Captured Allied soldiers were killed where they lay wounded, whilst the ones who had surrendered were also murdered.

The combined British forces withdrew across the causeway that separates Malaya from Singapore, and General Percival spread his troops across what must have been a sixty-mile stretch along the island's coastline. Whatever criticisms might later be attached to this strategy, the outcome could only have been the same.

The Japanese attacked across the Johore Strait but the Commonwealth troops were too spread out to affect the outcome. The Japanese entered the Alexandra Military Hospital and murdered any patients they found there. The nurses were raped and then murdered. The Japanese took almost 100,000 men prisoner in Singapore, many of whom hadn't even fired a shot in anger. A large number of these prisoners, perhaps 10,000, were later to die in constructing the Burma-Thailand railway.

The occupied people of Singapore were to be treated far worse. Those of Chinese origin were rounded up and slaughtered. It is estimated that as many as 50,000 perished in this manner.

Churchill had issued a directive to the army that there must be no thought of sparing either the troops or population, and that the senior officers should die alongside their troops, to uphold the honour of the British Empire and that of the Army.

The scrambling nets were draped over the side and the landing craft came alongside. Suddenly there was no war to fight. The atom bombs dropped on Hiroshima and Nagasaki brought the war to an abrupt end, with the unconditional surrender of Japanese forces in all theatres.

We still went into Malaya and Singapore though, but as liberators and occupational forces. The Japanese must have been practising their bowing, for wherever we went they were submissive, and we were quick to use them for manual labour and menial work.

Admiral Lord Louis Mountbatten, surrounded by a guard of honour of Royal Marines, read the proclamation from the steps of Government House and accepted the Japanese surrender.

We ourselves, 691 Flotilla, suddenly had no war to fight, and we were sent off to HMS *Terror*, a land-based naval camp, from where we were able to enjoy the delights of Singapore.

The jail at Changi where the Commonwealth prisoners were concentrated, was entered, and all the personnel were evacuated to various hospitals. It wasn't until we saw the state of most of them that we had difficulty in keeping our hands off the guards. Sufficient to say the commandant was subsequently hanged, but that didn't excuse the sadistic guards.

Camp routine was soon in place and the prospect of being demobbed was uppermost in everyone's mind. We had all been allocated our own demob numbers, based on age and length of service; they were posted on the noticeboard once a week and very carefully scanned.

Those eligible were given days to pack before they were shipped back to Blighty. I was on duty at the guardroom checking out those permitted to go on shore leave into Singapore or across to the island of Blakang Mati and because of this duty had refused, reluctantly, to go with my mates, and had reason to be thankful later when a number of them failed to return at 23:59 hours.

One of my close friends, who was celebrating his twenty-first birthday, had taken a drink of the local spirits marked as whiskey, that had been deliberately mixed with wood alcohol, and he and some of his friends had ended up in hospital, where he died.

Military funerals were something that no one looked forward to, having lived through the tremendous events of the last few years; it didn't make sense that traders could be so avaricious in the pursuit of a few dollars as to put such poison into anonymous drinks.

When we went ashore in future, we would stick to the two big amusement centres, The Happy World and The Great World. Here we found all the native eating houses and all the local traders that we could want. We chose a few mementos that we considered worth taking home.

Another good evening out was at the Cathay Cinema, where the military were able to obtain a concessionary ticket for $2.50. Then down to Lavender Street for a slap-up meal at Lucille. These places had been recommended and were found to be top notch.

We were only marking time, though, until our age and service number was posted on the noticeboard to announce our demob, and then we said our goodbyes and swapped addresses, promising to keep in touch.

Lt. Tighe, of course, being a regular, wasn't concerned with demob numbers, so he could expect a posting to 'Big Ships' again, now that the need for basic combined operations was over. However, rapid response seemed to be the way things were heading, so some kind of inter-service cooperation would probably be deemed essential. No longer would the three services be seen as individuals, fighting their corners for funds.

We said our goodbyes and thanks to Lt. Tighe. Without him and his leadership we wouldn't be going home at all. There is a bond between men who have faced death, which neither time nor separation can diminish, and this bond is enshrined in memory and requires only a moment of quietude to relive it. We would never forget what we owed to Tighe.

We finally boarded our transport home from Malaya, HMS *Anson*, a 35,000-ton battleship, and being a signalman I had to work my passage by duty on the bridge. The signalmen taking the passage home only spoke to the yeoman so it became a lonely duty, and we were glad to be relieved to go below for a belated meal. We didn't expect a chummy chat with the captain or his officers on watch, but we didn't exist until the lights started winking their Morse code, when we wrote down what we had received and passed it on without any "kiss my ass" or acknowledgement whatever.

We called in at Colombo and were given three days' shore leave. However, we had to be back on board by 23:59 so from the time we went ashore with the liberty men at 13:30 we had about eight hours to see the sights. We found a nice eating place, the Nanking Hotel in Chatham Street, Fort. The local beer was a bit weak but if you had enough of it, it wasn't too bad. Aden came and went and we arrived at Port Said, Egypt, the largest ship to use the canal to date.

There was four days' leave at Malta and we anchored in Valetta harbour. The whole place had been severely bombed and we understood that King George VI had awarded the island the George Cross on April 15th 1942.

We climbed to the highest point overlooking the harbour and took photographs of the *Anson* anchored there, and very smart she looked too, with her awnings out, a perfect setting in the Grand Harbour. The Captain, E. S. Bell, CBRN, flying the flag of Vice Admiral Sir John Edleston, must have been very proud of her. Coincidentally, HMS *Sheffield*, nicknamed HMS *Shiny*, was also anchored there. The cruiser famous for her participation in the *Bismarck* and *Scharnhorst* sinkings, she was 'working up' before proceeding to the American and West Indies stations. We had many happy meetings ashore with their crew. One crew setting out on a new commission, and the other, us, going home to be decommissioned and demobbed.

Arriving at Plymouth, we went through the usual customs searches, but with a difference. We were lined up in three ranks on the dockside together with our duffel bags and cases. The customs officer called out, "Anyone with anything to declare, step forward."

After a little hesitation, about twenty of us out of some three hundred stepped out of line.

"OK," said the officer, "you can carry on. The rest of you empty your bags and cases."

Being apprehensive and reasonably honest we had got away with murder, although with our little pay we couldn't afford a great deal of contraband, but I was thinking of the twelve half-pound tins of Tickler cigarette rolling tobacco that was stashed in the bottom of my duffel bag that, due to the shortages ashore, was worth a small fortune.

Handing back the military kit and small arms took little time at all and we were duly Signed Off, Decommissioned, Kaput, Not Wanted, Surplus to Requirements, Time Expired. Finito.

We made our way to a large warehouse, where we were allowed to choose a demob suit, shoes and all the bits that went with it.

A railway ticket and a handshake later we were standing on the pavement. Once again the umbilical of security and routine had been cut, leaving the new civilians with the need to think for themselves and to be responsible for their own actions.

Catching a train to the Midlands I leaned back on the seat and closed my eyes. So the great adventure was over. I was five years older. What was I going home to? What were we all going to do?

Had it all been worth it?

Only time would tell.

At least I was going home; a lot of my good friends hadn't made it.

God make their sacrifice worthwhile.

The conductor would wake me up at Snow Hill, Birmingham. My parents had moved from Brown Edge in the Potteries to find work whilst I had been away.

Britain was not the country that I had left all those years ago. She had exhausted herself in the pursuit of victory and had finally emerged into a period of complete austerity. Everything was strictly rationed – food, clothes, coal, even cigarettes and beer – and would probably remain so for the foreseeable future.

The first priority would be to look for a job, but we were in uniform and no longer needed by our country, and would be resented by being back on the job market. We were looked up to whilst we were fighting a war to keep the country safe, but with thousands of us back seeking work it posed a lot of problems. Our old jobs had been filled long before, and although firms were obliged by law to keep a job open for returning forces, in practice it didn't happen.

The government in its wisdom gave us three months' paid leave and kept us on the reserve for a number of years in case hostilities broke out again. However, what could I say at a job interview, when a prospective employer asked what I had to offer? "Well, sir, during the last five years I learned to kill with rifle, bayonet, crossbow, knife and my bare hands. I think I'm just the chap you are looking for in your accounts department." I'm sure the interview would end somewhat prematurely.

Still, no use looking on the dark side. The sun is shining, it's a lovely day, and in a few minutes I shall be reunited with my family and hopefully taking up with the lovely girl I left behind so many years ago.

So bring on the next challenge – the rest of life itself. Another great adventure was beginning.

PER MARE PER TERRAM

I never knew an appeal to them, for honour, courage, or loyalty, that they did not more than realise my highest expectations. If ever the hour of real danger should come to England, they will be found the Country's Sheet Anchor.

ADMIRAL LORD ST. VINCENT.